HONEYSUCKLE HOUSE

After nearly twenty-five years of marriage, Rosa's life seemed to be falling apart. Her husband, Leon, was leaving, her three children were unsettled, even her beloved home, Honeysuckle House, was at risk. Without Leon, the family was going to find it hard to cope with the running of Cookery Nook, the busy restaurant they had built up over the years from a run-down tea-shop. However, although Rosa could never have imagined it, Leon's leaving wasn't an end but a new beginning . . .

CHRISTINA JONES

HONEYSUCKLE HOUSE

Complete and Unabridged

LINFORD
Leicester

First published in Great Britain in 1995

First Linford Edition
published 2004

British Library CIP Data

Jones, Christina, *1948 –*
    Honeysuckle house.—
    Large print ed.—
    Linford romance library
    1. Love stories
    2. Large type books
    I. Title
    823.9′14 [F]

    ISBN 1–84395–533–4

Published by
F. A. Thorpe (Publishing)
Anstey, Leicestershire

Set by Words & Graphics Ltd.
Anstey, Leicestershire
Printed and bound in Great Britain by
T. J. International Ltd., Padstow, Cornwall

This book is printed on acid-free paper

The Letter

Rosa knew what was in the envelope
even before she picked it up from the
mat.

It lay there, protruding from the
usual morning thump of post, in a
shaft of early sunlight on the tiled hall
floor. A medium-sized, cream envelope
with the increasingly familiar logo of
Brennan and Foulkes, addressed to
Leon, her husband.

'Anything for me, Mum?'

She scooped up the letters just as
Kizzy appeared at the top of the stairs,
and pushed the cream envelope to the
bottom of the pile.

'One with an Edinburgh postmark.'
She smiled at her daughter, the smile
betraying none of the fear the cream
envelope had created. 'Just for a change . . . '

'Thanks, Mum!' Kizzy's beam chal-
lenged the sunshine. 'Only another

week and he'll be home!'

'And you'll have nothing left to talk about,' Rosa teased. 'Having written twice a day and lived on the phone every night . . . '

'Andrew and I always have things to talk about,' Kizzy retorted with eighteen-year-old superiority, as she disappeared back upstairs in a flurry of stripey nightshirt and tumbled red hair to read Andrew's latest missive in the privacy of her room.

Oh yes, Rosa thought, leafing quickly through the rest of the letters, keeping Brennan and Foulkes at the bottom, how well I remember being eighteen and in love.

Nearly twenty-five years ago, she and Leon had been just like Kizzy and Andrew, dreaming of their future, the whole world out there to conquer, and nothing mattering as long as they were together. And now . . .

Now, the regular letters from Brennan and Foulkes were a tangible reminder of just how wide the chasm had become.

'Anything interesting in the post?' Leon said artlessly, not looking up from his combination of the morning paper and a cup of tea as Rosa walked into the sunny dining-room.

'A letter from Andrew for Kizzy.' She walked to the window and looked out over her beloved garden. 'The usual circulars, a bank statement for William — and this . . . ' She turned slowly, holding out the cream envelope as though it physically burned her.

'Oh — right . . . ' Leon took the envelope, not meeting her eyes, and placed it unopened beneath his newspaper.

'You're not even going to open it?'

'Not yet.'

No, Rosa thought, watching him bend his head over the latest political scandal, not while I'm here. Whatever Brennan and Foulkes had to say, it didn't concern her.

'Leon, we have to discuss this . . . '

He looked up at her. 'Why? Discussion never seems to come into it, Rosa.

You're usually determined not even to consider it. This is it as far as you're concerned, isn't it?' He made a wide gesture round the high-ceilinged room. 'This house, the garden, the children, this tiny unfashionable town . . . Life begins and ends here for you, doesn't it?'

'Yes!' His words didn't even hurt her any more. 'Yes, it does! Leon, this is what we dreamed of, what we planned for. Half the couples in the country would give their eye teeth for what we've got here and — '

'And what finances it?' He leaned forward across the breakfast table. 'What has financed every home we've had, right from that first poky flat down on Mitchford Road, then the semi in the Crescent when William was a baby and Kizzy was on the way and we needed more space, then this . . . ?'

He stopped and looked around the tall room, with its bay window, its old-fashioned dado rails, its much-polished heavy furniture. It was almost as though he hated it, Rosa thought sadly. Almost as though he thought of Honeysuckle House as a prison. The house which had once been their joint dream . . .

'Cookery Nook.' Leon answered his own question, his eyes softening as he looked at Rosa. 'Cookery Nook, Rosa. We've built Cookery Nook up from a run-down tea-shop into a restaurant that features in all the main eating guides. And if we go ahead with this venture it could bring us — '

'No.' Rosa pulled up a chair across from her husband at the polished walnut table and poured a cup of tea. 'Listen to yourself, Leon. You're saying 'we' and 'us'. That means joint decisions, joint discussions. But you went ahead with this without even consulting me.'

'I didn't think you'd mind.' He folded the newspaper noisily. 'You used to back me one hundred per cent. It never occurred to me that you'd become so — so staid . . . '

'Staid!' She returned her cup to its saucer with a clatter. 'You think that wanting to stay here in Highcliffe where we know everyone and where our children have grown up, in this house, and run Cookery Nook — which has survived and prospered despite the recession — is staid?'

'Yes, I do! Look, Rosa, the Nook has gone as far as I can push it. There's no challenge any more. I set the same menus, create the same dishes, welcome the same clientele. To be honest, I'm bored . . . '

He gathered up his newspaper and the unopened letter from Brennan and Foulkes, and stalked from the dining-room.

★   ★   ★

She bit her lip. She loved him. And, more than that, she knew him, too well. They'd been married for nearly twenty-five years, and in that time she'd watched his enthusiasm for new ventures flare like embryo fires, and die just as quickly. But this . . . this was different.

She ran her fingers through her brown hair. Staid. Bored. They were words Leon was using with increasing regularity. Words calculated to wound — or at least cause a reaction.

'Mum! Where are you?'

Quickly Rosa wiped the tears from her lashes and stood up, her back to the door, again looking out over the garden while she composed herself.

'I'm in the dining-room, William. There's some tea in the pot but the toast's cold . . . '

'I'm not hungry, thanks . . . '

Rosa could hear her elder son pouring tea, could picture his tall, broad-shouldered frame lowering itself into Leon's chair — the carver that all three children had squabbled over for as long as she could remember.

'You were late last night . . . ' Still she gazed out across her garden.

'Spying on me, were you?' William

asked good-naturedly.

'No. I couldn't sleep ... ' She couldn't remember when she had last slept the night through. 'Was it a late night at the Nook?'

'Very.' William gulped his tea gratefully. 'One of the waitresses didn't turn up and the girl they sent from the agency was hopelessly slow. Then the two blokes who do the pot washing had a row and both walked out! If it hadn't been for Steven I'd have still been there now!'

'What was Steven doing at the Nook?' Rosa turned from the window. Steven Casey had been a friend of Leon's — and hers — since the early days, and Leon hadn't mentioned his presence. But then, Leon mentioned very little to her these days.

'He came in to see Dad.' William stretched out his long legs under the table. 'With one of his girlfriends in tow, of course. He begged a table and stayed anyway — and was I glad he did! He washes dishes like a dream!'

'What do you mean, he stayed anyway . . . ' Rosa felt the fear gnawing at her again. 'Didn't Dad sort things out? He didn't come home until at least half an hour after you . . . '

There was a silence as William suddenly seemed to find the dregs of his tea-cup extremely interesting.

'William . . . ?'

Rosa watched as her son struggled, her heart going out to him.

'Dad — Dad left the Nook sometime between seven and eight . . . I assumed he'd come here. I mean, he didn't say anything . . . ' He raised his blue eyes to his mother. 'To be honest, Mum, he's not at the Nook very often these days . . . I think he's lost interest.

'I mean, he leaves it more and more to me — the menus, the cooking. Then he just swans in at the end to chat to the diners and take the credit . . . '

Rosa winced at the bitterness in her son's voice.

'But not last night?'

'No. We had a full house and I was

literally left playing chief cook and bottle washer! I even had to go out in my whites and talk to Mr and Mrs Beatty! I wish you'd talk to Dad, Mum.'

Talk to him, Rosa thought, her heart growing heavier by the second. When did the talking stop and the bickering start? What on earth had happened to her marriage? To the happy-go-lucky dreamer she had married?

'I'll talk to him . . . ' She tried to smile. 'But at least it shows that he trusts you to run the Nook single-handed, doesn't it? He's acknowledging that you're as good a chef as he is . . . '

'I'll never be that.' William poured another cup of tea. 'I don't have his flair. I still cook from recipes — Dad creates food from his heart . . . '

'True.' Rosa sighed. 'He's a genius in the kitchen. But what on earth did Mr and Mrs Beatty say when you appeared in full garb?'

'Nothing much.' William grinned,

relieved that Rosa hadn't cross-questioned him about Leon's absence. 'I told them that Dad had been called away. They asked after you, though,' he finished hurriedly.

'I'll probably call in today.'

Rosa smoothed her sweatshirt down over her jeans, her calm, unlined face not betraying her pain. Paul Beatty was their bank manager, his wife, Norma, shared her passion for gardening, and they had become firm friends of the family.

She walked towards the door, then turned. 'William, what do you know about Brennan and Foulkes?'

'Brennan and who?' He shook his head. 'Never heard of them. Which team do they play for?'

'They don't!' Rosa managed to laugh. At least William was being kept in the dark, too. 'I think they're financial consultants . . . '

'You ought to ask the Beattys, then. They're sure to know. I'm the last person to ask about finance — my bank statement is screaming scarlet!'

'Yes, I might just do that . . . ' Rosa mused.

★   ★   ★

William leaned back in the carver as Rosa closed the door and let out his breath with a sigh. He'd always taken his parents' relationship for granted, but there was something wrong somewhere. His mother seemed sad, distant, while his father . . . He shook his head. His father's bright-eyed, almost fevered, joie-de-vivre was even more worrying. And his sudden lack of interest at Cookery Nook was fuelling a fever of lurid staff-room rumours.

The dining-room door suddenly crashed open, and Kizzy flew in, still in her nightshirt, with her hair tumbling across her face.

'I thought Mum was in here.'

'She was. I think she's on the phone. Why?'

Kizzy waved a sheaf of pages beneath her brother's nose.

'Andrew's letter! He'll be home next week — fully qualified! We're getting married!'

★   ★   ★

Leon Brodie straightened his tie and ran his fingers through his hair in the driving mirror. The car park was full, each space being filled immediately it became vacant by another harassed driver.

He glanced at his watch. He was still too early, so, settling back in his seat, he tried to watch the comings and goings around him. It was mostly women at this time of the afternoon, women with children, loading bags of supermarket shopping into the backs of cars. Why was it a source of irritation to him that Rosa didn't drive?

'I'm just not co-ordinated!' She'd laughed years ago when he'd tried to teach her. 'It'll be safer for all concerned if I stay on my feet or my bicycle!'

He'd tried several more times, each time more disastrous than the last, and they'd always ended up laughing like hysterical children over Rosa's inability to change gear, steer and watch the road at the same time.

Leon glanced at his watch again. Ten minutes to go.

That laughter — it seemed like a lifetime ago, he thought with sadness. How long was it since he had heard Rosa laugh? When was the last time *he* had laughed at Honeysuckle House . . . ?

Getting out of the car, he brushed down his suit jacket, and the envelope from Brennan and Foulkes rustled warningly in his breast pocket.

'Oh, Rosa . . . ' He sighed. 'Why are you fighting me on this? Don't you realise what you're doing?'

Striding across the car park towards the glass-fronted office block, he felt a sudden pang of guilt. He shouldn't have been so sharp this morning. He'd hurt her — and he loved her still, in a way.

Even before he'd told Rosa that he needed to sell the Nook, the house, move out of Highcliffe and achieve his final dream before it was too late, he was aware that he loved her out of habit.

She was there — and if she wasn't there he would miss her terribly — but the fire had gone out, and there was no enthusiasm left to fan the embers and create even a flickering glow.

He dismissed the thought that he was trying to justify himself as he smiled at Brennan and Foulkes's pretty receptionist.

'One moment, Mr Brodie.' She smiled back. 'Miss Phelps is on the phone but she's expecting you. Would you like to take a seat?'

Sitting in the chrome and glass reception area, Leon looked at the rainforest greenery and the abstract paintings in ocean shades of blue and grey.

Rosa had always loved the sea. That was why she was so delighted with Honeysuckle House, because it stood proudly on the clifftop and she could watch the waves from at least ten of its windows.

She had been like a child that day they'd moved in, running from room to room, and always pausing at the huge sashed windows to look at the sea.

But the new place was only just around the bay; they could buy another house, more modern, less work, with just such a view; maybe better.

But Rosa refused to listen. Refused to budge.

'Mr Brodie? So sorry to have kept you . . . ' The slightly husky voice jolted his heart, and Leon stood up, knowing that his smile was just too wide for a client meeting his financial adviser, yet unable to help himself.

'Good afternoon, Miss Phelps.' His brown eyes held hers as his hand closed over cool, slender fingers in a polite handshake. 'I'm sorry if I'm early . . . '

'No problem.' Felicity Phelps returned his smile and turned to the receptionist. 'Hold my calls, Nicky. Mr Brodie and I will be in conference for about an hour. We don't want to be disturbed.'

Leon held open the door, and followed Felicity Phelps up the open-plan staircase to her office. He tried not to stare at her long elegant legs in the high-heeled court shoes, or the way her slenderness was accentuated by the expensively-cut pale grey suit, or the way her heavy honey-coloured hair was gathered into a neat roll at the nape of her neck.

Felicity Phelps was the most beautiful woman he had ever met.

Her office was at the front of the building, overlooking the town square.

'So?' She looked at him from those clear hazel eyes, fringed with naturally dark lashes. 'Any change?'

'None.' Leon shook his head. Neither of them had sat down. 'I didn't even show her your proposals this morning.

We managed to row about the letter before I'd even opened the envelope.'

'And you're determined to go ahead with the plan? Even without your wife's consent to sell Cookery Nook?'

'Yes.' Leon swallowed.

'Even if it means forcing her to sell her shares in the business? To sell your home? To mortgage everything you've got to achieve it?'

'Yes.'

Felicity Phelps walked over to her window, and leaned her beautifully-manicured hands on the sill. Leon loosened his tie.

When he'd first come here, to Brennan and Foulkes, just after Christmas, when he'd told Rosa of his plans and she'd refused point blank even to consider them, he'd thought F. Phelps and the string of letters after the name indicated someone like Paul Beatty; an ageing financial wizard who would peer at him over half-moon glasses and tell him he was out of his mind.

He had been totally unprepared for

the cool, elegant intelligence of this beautiful woman. Totally unprepared for her sharp business brain, her acumen, her insight. Totally unprepared to fall in love.

'Felicity . . . '

She turned from the window, her eyes gentle.

'No questions about last night?'

Leon shook his head. 'None. Rosa was asleep when I got in.'

'And William?'

'William just accepted that I was going out. I felt rotten about it, because the Nook was full, but he can cope. He's an excellent chef, and never loses his head in a crisis.'

'Unlike you.'

'Unlike me but like Rosa.' Leon grinned. 'Jamie takes after me. Impetuous, wanting everything — and wanting it now! Kizzy has inherited a combination of both our characters, making her a sensible dreamer, with her head in the clouds and her feet on the ground.'

'It sounds like an ideal combination

to me.' Felicity moved across the office towards him. 'And what's she going to do with her life?'

'A-levels this summer, then university, then teaching. Kizzy knows exactly what she's going to do with her life. I wish I did . . . '

'Poor Leon.' Felicity looked at him with genuine concern. 'You really didn't want this to happen, did you?'

'I never dreamed it would.' Leon held her hands in his. 'This isn't a fling, for me, Felicity. I've never been in love with anyone but Rosa . . . '

'And you still are.' Felicity studied their linked hands. 'Aren't you?'

'Yes.' Leon freed one hand to stroke her cheek. 'I still love Rosa. But not like this. I've never felt like this in my life . . . '

'Neither have I.' Her voice was taut. 'I was too busy with my career to have time for any man. And now here I am, hopelessly in love with a married man of fifty with three children . . . '

They stared at each other in silence

for a moment, then Felicity pulled away.

'Business, Mr Brodie. You've studied the proposals?'

'Yes. I understand the implications. If Rosa agrees to sell the shares in Cookery Nook and sell the house, then Brennan and Foulkes are prepared to source additional financial backing to get the Four Seasons off the ground?'

'I've sounded out some of my investors.' Felicity perched on the edge of the desk, crossing slender ankles. 'And there is certainly some interest in providing an upmarket country club in Dawley. They like the idea of a hotel, restaurant, leisure complex and conference hall all under one roof.'

'Hence the Four Seasons.' Leon's eyes shone with enthusiasm. 'Oh, if only Rosa knew what she's throwing away!'

In more ways than one, Felicity Phelps thought sadly, looking at the animated face of the man who was surely going to break her heart.

* ★ ★ ★

James Brodie kicked his trainered feet
aimlessly against the wall. Maybe this
hadn't been such a brilliant idea after
all.

Dawley on a mid-week afternoon was
not the most exciting place in the world
— although it certainly had more going
for it than dreary old Highcliffe where
there really was nothing to do. But, he
shrugged his thin shoulders, what was
the point of bunking off school when all
his friends were still diligently in the
classroom and the last of his money had
been fed into the greedy mouths of the
slot machines in the sea-front arcade? It
hadn't taken long to get through it. He
didn't even have his bus-fare, and
twelve miles to walk home was pretty
daunting, even for someone who could
run for ever when playing football for
the school team.

He jumped from the car park wall
and began to make his way towards the
main road. He couldn't hitch a lift

22

— Mum and Dad would kill him if they found out! And there was enough trouble at home without him causing any more.

As he crossed the car park, he saw a familiar car and wandered towards it. Yes, it was Dad's! Brilliant! He'd hang around and get a lift.

He leaned against the bonnet, much more cheerful now. He'd tell Dad that he'd been on a field trip to Dawley with his study group and he'd got separated. Dad was so funny these days, always miles away, he'd believe anything.

'Jamie!'

He jumped guiltily at the sound of his name. It wasn't one of his teachers, was it? His luck couldn't be that bad! He squinted against the sun.

'Jamie? Do you want a lift back to Highcliffe? Or are you waiting for someone?'

'Oh, hi, Mr Casey . . . ' Jamie grinned. This was even better. Steven Casey, even though he was friends with Mum and Dad, always seemed so much younger. Artistic, Kizzy said. Whatever it was, he knew that he wouldn't ask any awkward questions. 'Yeah — please.'

He scrambled into Steven's ancient car, piled as usual with books and boxes and odd bits of china. A jumble sale on wheels, Kizzy had once said.

'Home or school?' Steven asked as they pulled out of the car park.

'Home, please.'

They exchanged conspiratorial grins.

'Tough being fourteen, isn't it?' Steven asked as they pulled out into the main road.

But Jamie wasn't listening. He'd just seen his father come out of one of the new office buildings, and he wasn't alone. Who was the blonde lady in the suit who got into the car with him? For the first time it struck Jamie to wonder why his father wasn't at the Nook . . .

'Was that your father's car you were leaning against?' Steven drove very fast. 'Were you waiting for him?'

'Dad?' Jamie thought quickly. 'No. I

thought it was his car — but it wasn't
. . . same make and colour . . . '

'Ah . . . ' Steven said and turned up
the stereo to full volume.

'If I drop you along Sea Road,' he
raised his voice above the blast of the
stereo, 'you can walk from there and get
in about your usual time . . . '

'Great!' Jamie beamed at him. 'You're
ace, Mr Casey!'

'I'm a reprobate who hasn't
grown-up — you ask your mother.'
Steven laughed at him. 'And I think the
least said about this, the better, don't
you?'

'Sure,' Jamie said, as he opened the
door. 'Thanks again, Mr Casey.'

Once the car had disappeared from
sight along Sea Road in a cloud of dust,
Jamie slowed his pace to an amble. He
was in no hurry to get home. The
atmosphere there was hopeless these
days.

Dad was never there, and Mum
always looked like she'd been awake
half the night. William was worrying

himself silly about keeping the Nook going and being as good as Dad, and Kizzy just moped about Andrew being hundreds of miles away in Scotland. None of them had any time for him.

'Jamie Brodie!'

This time the voice was female. Jamie closed his eyes. Please don't let it be Miss Jenkins, the Deputy Head. Anyone but her . . .

'Jamie!' The voice was peremptory.

Saved again, Jamie thought with relief as he saw Norma Beatty waving to him over the top of her hedge.

'Could you give us a hand, dear?'

''Course I can . . . ' Jamie's smile was genuinely warm. He liked Mr and Mrs Beatty. They were like substitute grand-parents. He'd never known his own. He trotted through the gate into the garden.

'What do you want me to do?'

'Your mum came to admire the garden and as usual got carried away! She could do with a pair of strong arms to help her carry the cuttings home.

And,' Norma's eyes twinkled, 'I'm sure if you pop into the kitchen you'll find a packet of crisps and some cola in the larder . . . '

'Thanks, Mrs Beatty!' Jamie dashed off in search of refreshment. Maybe today wasn't so bad after all.

Norma Beatty returned to the bottom of the garden and rejoined Rosa on the weathered bench beneath a gnarled apple tree.

'Just collared your Jamie.' She sighed contentedly. 'Must have been on his way home from school. He's having something to eat and then he'll help you carry everything home.'

'Thanks.' Rosa smiled at the older woman. 'It's at times like this that I wish I could drive.'

'Nonsense — you carry on with your walking and cycling and you'll keep your teenage figure until you're ninety!' Norma's laugh gurgled up through the branches of the tree. 'You don't look old enough to have three children, my dear.'

'I feel like Methuselah at the moment,' Rosa admitted. 'My whole life seems to have turned upside down. Are you sure Leon hasn't approached Paul?'

'You know I couldn't discuss bank business — even if I knew. But I'm sure of one thing. If he has told Paul his plans to sell Cookery Nook and Honeysuckle House, Paul would have advised very strongly against it.'

'So, he's gone elsewhere for the answer he wants.' Rosa sighed. 'He'll never change. They used to be one of his most attractive qualities — his impossible dreams. But now — ' Her voice caught in her throat. 'Now, they just seem foolish . . . '

'Men often go through this sort of thing at his age,' Norma said sagely. 'It's a last-ditch grab at their fading youth.' She squeezed her friend's tightly-clenched hands.

'Let it ride its course. Common sense will prevail in the end . . . '

Maybe, Rosa thought, but this idea of

Leon's wasn't just a whim. This was a full-blown business plan, and with strong encouragement from Brennan and Foulkes he was going to see it through — with or without her.

And, of course, there was something else . . . Intuitively, she knew there was something else . . .

Jamie, fully replete, wandered into the garden to seek out his mother.

'Hello, darling.' She smiled at him. 'Good day?'

'Bits of it . . . ' he answered honestly.

'Good.' Her eyes were distracted, and he breathed a sigh of relief. 'I won't be long.'

'Steven Casey was in the Nook last night,' Norma Beatty said as she stood up. 'Did William tell you?'

'Yes.' Rosa nodded. 'With a new lady, I understand.'

'Very glamorous.' Norma laughed. 'Not a local. I don't suppose he'll ever settle down. Now there's a prime example of a man clinging to his youth if ever I saw one!'

Jamie swallowed the words that had bubbled on to his tongue. He'd just about said that Steven Casey had given him a lift home from Dawley!

He half-listened to his mother's and Mrs Beatty's disjointed conversation as they gathered the plants together. Boring talk, most of it, to do with Steven Casey and his girlfriends. Then, something else.

' . . . so, no more fretting about Brennan and Foulkes,' Mrs Beatty was saying. 'I'm sure it'll all blow over . . . '

'Oh!' Jamie looked up at his mother. 'I saw . . . '

'What, darling?'

'Nothing . . . nothing . . . ' Jamie mumbled, blushing, suddenly becoming very engrossed in a clump of clover.

Brennan and Foulkes was the name over the office block that Dad had come out of with that blonde woman . . .

A War Of Words

Did her whole family communicate via notes on the pin board these days? Rosa stared in exasperation at Kizzy's, 'Won't be in for dinner. Gone to Andrew's mum's. GOT to talk to you and Dad TONIGHT! You'd disappeared this morning. Loads of love, K.'

William's, 'Gone to the Nook. Some crisis. Tell Dad', was short and to the point. Meanwhile, Jamie had shut himself in his room with two school-friends and some unfathomable computer game.

What was happening to her family? There didn't seem to be a minute for them all to be together to talk. And they had to talk. Desperately.

She heard Leon's car scrunch into the gravelled drive, and quickly hurried to the mirror. Her hair was slightly dishevelled, her face shiny from her exertions in the garden, planting her collection of cuttings. But her hair still had no trace of grey, and her figure was trim. She hadn't let herself go.

'I'm in the kitchen,' she called, hearing Leon's key in the lock. 'Is the crisis sorted out now?'

'Crisis? What crisis?' Leon appeared in the doorway.

Rosa looked up quickly. 'William left a note.' She indicated the pin board. 'I thought you'd gone down to sort it out.'

'No . . . ' He didn't meet her eyes. 'I've been out. On business. I haven't been into the Nook yet. I'll ring him.'

'Ring him? Leon, you'll go down there and help him!' Her voice was more strident than she had intended. 'He can't carry it all on his own! He's a wonderful chef, but he's no restaurateur! You're not being fair!'

'And you know all about fairness, I suppose? You think that it's fair to block my plans without even considering them?'

'That's not what we're talking about!'

Rosa swallowed. She had to diffuse this before it developed into yet another row. She went on more quietly. 'We're talking about our son and what you're expecting him to do.'

'All I'm expecting him to do is what I had to do at his age. Don't mollycoddle him so much, Rosa. I'll go down to the Nook later.'

He looked at his wife and suddenly felt like crying. 'You've got dirt on your nose . . . '

'I've been gardening . . . '

They looked at each other for a long time without speaking. They were like strangers, each carefully considering their words so as not to antagonise the other, when at one time they would have laughed and shouted, argued and loved, without a second thought.

'The letter,' Rosa turned back towards the sink, 'from Brennan and Foulkes. Is that where you've been?'

'Yes.'

'And is that where you went last night when the Nook was a waitress short and William had to get Steven to help with the pot washing?'

There was a silence that roared in her ears.

'I left before the row in the kitchen. I got a waitress from the agency — I didn't know she was going to be hopeless. And yes, that's where I went . . . '

'I won't sell my shares in the Nook, Leon, and I will not agree to sell Honeysuckle House. We're too old for hare-brained ventures now.'

'You may be too old, Rosa, but I'm not.' His tone tore at her heart. 'The Old Granary will be perfect for the Four Seasons — just come and have a look . . . '

'No.' She turned from the sink. 'I've supported you in every decision you've made in the past, maybe stamped on some of the crazier ones, and always been prepared to produce business plans, work out finance, chat to whoever was necessary . . . ' Her eyes misted. 'You used to say that you were the doer and I was the thinker — and that was the combination that got us the Nook. What's happened to us?'

'Nothing.' There was a note of irritation in his voice. 'At least, not to me. I just think that being fifty isn't a signal for pipe, slippers and early retirement, that's all.'

'I'm forty-seven, and I don't think like that either. But the children — '

'The children will make their own way, like we did. William will leave the Nook and probably run some cosy little eaterie in London. Kizzy will become a teacher and live miles away from us. And Jamie — ' He gave a snort. 'Jamie will probably be scoring the winning goal in the Cup Final in five years' time and forget that he's even got parents!'

'You know very well that that's nonsense!'

'I seem to talk nothing but nonsense these days, don't I? Rosa, please . . . Tomorrow, come with me to view the Old Granary.'

'No, Leon. No.'

She clenched her hands tightly as he turned on his heel and marched across the hall, slamming the front door on his way out.

Leon glanced at his car in the drive and decided to walk. He didn't trust himself to drive at the moment. Always careful behind the wheel, he knew that his current anger might well lead him to throw caution to the winds.

He shivered inside his jacket as the wind whipped up from the sea in the gathering dusk. He hadn't wanted that argument. He'd planned to walk in and take Rosa in his arms and try to persuade her with gentle words, the way he'd used to. But she hadn't allowed him to.

Felicity's beautiful face danced inside his head and the pain was almost intolerable. How on earth had he got into this mess?

He turned into the High Street, striding briskly towards the Nook. The Nook — once his pride and joy — now felt like a millstone round his neck.

Kizzy, cycling back from Andrew's parents, watched her father disappear into the Nook, and sighed heavily. She really needed to talk to them together. Now it would have to be just Mum and that was going to be more difficult. She had always been able to twist her father round her little finger.

Never mind, at least Andrew's parents had thought it was a wonderful idea. And she was eighteen. She was an adult. She could do what she wanted. Of course, it would be better to have Mum and Dad's blessing, but if they refused, she'd go ahead anyway . . .

★   ★   ★

'Married?' Rosa's eyebrows rocketed into her hairline. 'How lovely, Kizzy! When did he propose?'

'In the letter this morning . . . ' Kizzy grinned. This was going better than she had ever dreamed. 'I came down to tell you, but you'd already gone out. Andrew's parents think it's great. He's

37

fully qualified now, and his father will make him a partner in the market garden and — '

'We'll have an engagement party at the Nook.' Rosa felt as though a weight had been lifted from her heart. 'Like we did for your eighteenth birthday.' This would surely take Leon's mind off buying the Old Granary and moving to Dawley. His only daughter becoming engaged to Andrew Pearson. 'And William can make the cake . . . '

'Mum — ' Kizzy held up her hands. 'We don't want an engagement party.'

'Oh, but you must! Are you going to wait until after your A-levels? That will give us nearly three months to get things organised . . . '

'No, Mum. We're not getting engaged.'

'But . . . You've just said . . . '

'I said Andrew had proposed. We're getting married, Mum, not engaged. We're getting married as soon as my exams are over . . . at the end of June.'

Rosa felt as though someone had just

punched all the breath from her body. Her head reeled.

'Kizzy, you can't! What about university? What about teaching? What about — ?'

'Oh, I can go to college any time once I've got my A-levels. I'll apply to somewhere nearer. I might not even want to. All I want to do is marry Andrew and — '

'Be divorced before you're twenty-one!' Rosa stared in disbelief at her daughter. 'Kizzy, you can't do this. Get engaged by all means. Go to college so you and Andrew will both be qualified. Then think about getting married! But not this — '

'Mum — ' Kizzy leaned forward. ' — I'm not asking you, I'm telling you. This is my life. Andrew's parents have been married for thirty years and they're still soppy about each other — and look at you and Dad. It'll soon be your Silver Wedding and you're still happy. That's what we want . . . '

'But university is — '

'You didn't go to college. Neither did Dad. And look how well you've done. No, Mum, we've made up our minds. I've even been to see the vicar. The church is booked for June twenty-fifth . . . '

Rosa reached out and took her daughter's hands, tears in her eyes.

'Kizzy, listen to me. Don't do this. We really like Andrew, but you're far too young at the moment. Have you spoken to Dad? I'm sure he'll — '

'He'll understand.' Kizzy smiled beguilingly. 'Look, Mum, we can live in the bungalow in the market garden — we won't even have to worry about a mortgage. It'll all work out brilliantly!'

'And what will you do? Help out in the market garden shop? With three A-levels?'

'Don't be such a snob!' Kizzy laughed. 'Jess Owen got four last year and she still works in the supermarket. Qualifications don't mean anything these days. All we want is to be together and be as happy as you are . . . '

Rosa bit her lip. Now was not the right time to tell her daughter that her parents' marriage was falling apart more painfully with each day.

'Mum, tell Dad for me, will you? He can get things moving at the Nook for the reception. I'm going to have a bath and an early night . . . ' She left the room quickly before Rosa could add to her arguments.

★   ★   ★

The darkening sitting-room seemed full of shadows. Rosa didn't switch on the lamps, but sat on the sofa, somehow comforted by the darkness.

Kizzy could marry whether she and Leon agreed or not. Marriage . . .

Rosa shook her head. She just couldn't let Kizzy go through the pain that she was experiencing. She would have to persuade her to re-think.

She stood up and moved over to the phone and quickly dialled the Nook.

'William? Sorry to ring at your busy

time, love. Could I have a word with Dad, please?'

Leon would agree that Kizzy must get her qualifications first, of that Rosa was sure. He was so proud of his daughter's academic achievements. And it wasn't as if they were going to block the wedding — only ask them to postpone it.

'Sorry? What? Well, when did he leave?' Her heart sank like a stone. 'OK, William. No — no problem. I'll speak to him when he comes in . . . '

Hugging her arms round her waist, Rosa wandered to the sitting-room window and stared out into the blackness of the evening. Somewhere out there the sea crashed ceaselessly on to the beach. Somewhere, Leon was laughing, talking, charming people as he had once charmed her.

Kizzy was at one end of the chain of love — while she was surely at the other. It was hard to know which was the more painful . . .

Hours later, Rosa was unable to

sleep. She had heard William come in just after one o'clock and go straight to his room, obviously exhausted by yet another night single-handed at the Nook. And Leon's car was still in the drive . . .

She'd had a bath, forced down a milky drink, tried to concentrate on a novel, but nothing worked. She felt as tense as a runner in the blocks waiting for the starter's pistol. Sleep was impossible. Relaxation was hopeless.

Where was Leon? She let her hand stray to the empty space beside her in the big double bed. It seemed like a huge void now. Cold.

With her stomach cramped in tight knots, she slid her feet to the floor and pattered to the window.

The street was quiet under the orange street light glow. No lights showed in the other houses. Highcliffe's residents slept snugly.

The moon drifted across a wine-dark sky, buffeted by the occasional black cloud.

Suddenly, white headlights sliced through the nocturnal solitude. The car purred to a halt outside and Rosa pulled the curtains aside. Maybe Steven had given Leon a lift home.

The car was long, low and opulent. Definitely not Steven's. Rosa watched as the passenger door opened and Leon, looking not a day older than William in the soft nightglow, slid out.

Rosa's heart fluttered. The tension inside began to lessen. At least he was home . . .

Closing the passenger door quietly, he moved round to the driver's side of the car and leaned in the window. The treacherous moon chose that moment to disperse the clouds and illuminate the street.

The driver of the car was young, beautiful and blonde. A stranger.

Rosa watched as Leon, her husband, leaned farther inside the car and kissed the blonde, beautiful stranger tenderly and with love.

Numb with shocked disbelief, Rosa

gripped the curtain between rigid fingers. Nausea rose in waves, roaring in her ears, paralysing her whole body. She'd known there was something . . . but not this. Never this!

In the glorious silver moonlight, the car slid away. Leon watched it until it turned the corner then moved towards the house.

Rosa was too horrified to cry; shout; to move even. She wanted to feel anger, but there was nothing, just the constricting of her throat and an iron band crushing her lungs. Her eyes were still drawn to the street, as if some miracle would rewind the whole awful scene and make it merely a bad dream.

Leon hesitated on the drive, glanced up towards the bedroom window, then hurried off down the road in the opposite direction from the car.

He knew he couldn't creep into Honeysuckle House, tip-toe up the stairs, and slide into bed beside Rosa as if nothing had happened. How could he, when Felicity's perfume still lingered on his clothes and her kiss still lingered on his lips? His wife deserved better than that.

Quickening his pace in the darkness, he wondered if he was alone in finding this sort of situation impossible to cope with. How did other men react? Did they all feel remorse and shame at the pain they were inflicting when they fell foolishly in love with someone else?

The shingled track scrunched beneath his feet as he ducked beneath overhanging trees to reach his destination. A light glowed dully in an upstairs room. Leon rapped on the door with relief.

'What the — ' Steven Casey, still fully dressed, pulled open the door and stared at his visitor. 'Leon! What's happened? Has Rosa — No, don't tell me, come in.'

Gratefully, Leon climbed the twisting wooden stairs to the flat above Steven's antiques shop. Once in the living-room, he turned to face his friend.

'I'm sorry. There was nowhere else I could go . . . '

'She knows, then?' Steven reached for two glasses and the whisky decanter and poured two large drinks. 'Well, don't say I didn't warn you. I've tried to tell you — '

'Rosa knows nothing.' Leon swallowed half the contents of his glass in one gulp. 'That's not why I'm here.'

'Then why?' Steven refilled the glass. 'It's a heck of a time for a social call!'

'I went out with Felicity tonight. We went for a meal in Dawley — I was checking out the opposition. Then we walked around the Old Granary — you know, the place I want to convert — in the moonlight, just visualising how it could be . . . '

'Leon — ' Steven cleared the sofa of second-hand books and two tabby cats and sat down 'Get the to point. I'm not interested in the hearts and flowers.'

Leon sank down beside him.

'It's just — each time I'm with her it feels more right . . . ' He sighed. 'I was late getting back . . . I couldn't go indoors. Rosa doesn't deserve this.'

'No, she doesn't,' Steven said. 'You're behaving like an idiot! You'll lose her, Leon. And if you do, you'll regret it for the rest of your life!'

'But the Four Seasons is my dream and Felicity has become part of it. You know, Steve, when I think of the Four Seasons, I see Felicity beside me, not Rosa . . . '

'Then you're a bigger idiot than I thought!' Steven exploded. 'Rosa and the kids are your reality, Leon, not some half-baked dream. OK, Felicity is a gorgeous lady, but so is Rosa. Stop all this nonsense — now.'

'That's rich coming from you!' Leon helped himself to another drink. 'You never keep the same woman in your life for more than a couple of months . . . '

'Ah, but I'm not married.' Steven squinted into his glass. 'And if I had a family like yours, I know I wouldn't be jeopardising it like this. Not for anything.

'I whisked young Jamie away from Brennan and Foulkes this afternoon just before you and Felicity appeared. If you're going to flaunt her, it might be a good idea not to do it in front of your children!'

'Oh.' Leon groaned. 'Why was Jamie in Dawley?'

'Why don't you ask him?' Steven stood up quickly. 'I doubt if you're at home often enough to ask any of your kids anything these days!

'There's a blanket in the airing cupboard — you can share the sofa with the cats — and first thing in the morning, go back to Honeysuckle House and grow up!'

Leon winced as the door slammed shut behind Steven. He hadn't expected sympathy — he knew the high regard in which his friend held Rosa — but understanding, yes. Wasn't there anyone who would understand?

He collected the blanket and pulled it over him, while the cats watched him from baleful amber eyes.

'Don't look at me like that,' Leon muttered at them. 'I'm not going to steal your bed for ever . . . '

With a sigh he buried his head in the musty cushions and heard St Peter's clock striking three.

★   ★   ★

Kizzy heard the chime of St Peter's and turned in her sleep. Church bells . . . wedding bells . . . In three months' time she would be the most beautiful bride Highcliffe had ever seen. She'd have to tell Dad in the morning.

Jamie snuggled beneath the duvet, listening to the church clock. Three o'clock — hours before he had to get up. The bells echoed away, reminding him of Christmas and childhood. Tomorrow he'd bunk off school after registration and go into Dawley again and try to win his money back in the arcade . . .

William tossed and turned, exhausted but unable to sleep. Lisa hadn't turned

50

in again tonight, and Dad hadn't stayed long enough to allow him to slip away. Why hadn't she answered the phone? Two nights running and she hadn't shown up. There was something very wrong. He'd have to find out tomorrow . . . Lisa might be just another waitress to Dad, but not to him.

He was so tired . . . so very tired . . .

One, two, three . . . Rosa listened to the shuddering chimes of St Peter's. How long before daybreak? Surely this horror would recede with the daylight?

Another woman. Had she driven Leon into the arms of another woman? A blonde, beautiful, rich woman.

Her mouth was dry and her head ached, but still she felt no anger. She felt pain and — guilt? Yes, she almost laughed . . . she felt guilty. There must be some reason why Leon wanted someone else — and that reason could only lie with her. Was she staid and boring, as he'd accused her? Was she complacently happy with her life? Was she so determined to keep things as they always had been that her plans to stifle this last outrageous scheme of Leon's had finally driven him away?

She looked round the darkened bedroom with its brass bed and its Victorian furniture, its china pitcher and ewer, its water colour paintings. This bedroom was hers and Leon's — and this was where he belonged.

Furiously, the anger finally swelled inside her and she grabbed her pillow.

'No, I'm not staid and boring! Yes, I'm happy with my life — or at least, I was! No, I'm not complacent! And yes, I'm going to keep things just as they've always been — Four Seasons, blonde beauties, or not! You've got a fight on your hands, Leon Brodie!'

She punched the pillow with each assertion, hot tears scalding her cheeks, then fell forward across the bed and wept quietly, until exhaustion swept her into oblivion.

Pain — And Guilt

William looked around the devastation of the dining-room with an air of resignation. The table was a mess of half-finished cups of coffee and toast crusts, and by the two places he guessed that his brother and sister had breakfasted alone and then rushed off to school without a second thought.

Helping himself to fresh coffee, he lowered himself into the carver. His parents' bedroom door had been firmly shut when he'd crossed the landing, so they were obviously having a lie-in for once.

He'd have to see Dad about the state of things at the Nook, of course, but he could wait. This morning he had more important things to sort out.

After clearing the dining-room table, he pulled on his denim jacket and stepped out into a typical damp morning. The rain was fine, a salt-spray mist gusted up from the sea, and he needed the windscreen wipers on the Mini as he drove along the High Street and turned towards the Common.

The houses here were tall and narrow, belonging to an earlier era of grace and gentility, and parking was difficult in the winding street.

He rang the bell at No. 22 and stepped back as the door was pulled open barely an inch.

'Yes?'

'I'd like to see Lisa Ross, please. I believe she rents a room here?'

'She does.' The middle-aged woman opened the door a fraction wider. 'She ain't in.'

'Could I wait, then?' William smiled politely.

'No point.' The landlady shook her head. 'I don't know when she'll be back. She's moving her stuff out — could be gone all day . . . '

'Moving? Where?'

'Don't know, and really I don't care.

Look, I don't want to sound hard, but rules is rules — and Lisa didn't stick to them. I gave her notice day before yesterday — and I didn't have to do that. After what she's done I could have asked her to leave immediately. As it was, I gave her till the end of the week. So, you see, you could be waiting all day. Sorry . . . ' And the door was firmly closed in his face.

Bewildered, William walked slowly back to his car, the rain trickling irritatingly down the neck of his jacket.

He sat inside, turning on the radio for company, but his thoughts soon blanked out the music. What on earth was Lisa up to?

The young waitress had worked at the Nook for nearly four months. Leon had taken her on and William had liked her immediately, not just because she was small and pretty with her long dark hair in a pony-tail, and a smile never far from her lips, but because she was genuinely interested in the Nook. So many of the waitresses were efficient and polite, and left the job behind the moment the last order had been served. But not Lisa. Lisa asked questions about the recipes, even made suggestions.

They had become friends through their mutual interest in the kitchen — and that laughing friendship had developed into something deeper.

Even so, Lisa remained something of a mystery, never volunteering any information about her past or her family.

But none of that mattered to William. Although she had always turned down his invitations to the cinema when their nights off coincided, and never invited him into her lodgings when he drove her home after work, still their relationship had deepened.

So what on earth had she done? What heinous crime had she committed that her landlady had felt obliged to throw her out? He couldn't imagine his happy, laughing, gentle Lisa ever doing anything to upset anyone. That was how he thought of her, he admitted to himself. His Lisa . . .

He was unsure of his next move. Should he wait a bit longer and see if she returned, or should he go back home and tackle Dad over the Nook?

Ruefully he shook his head. Not the latter. Best leave Mum and Dad on their own for a while longer.

The rain had melted into a sea-fret and a watery sun was peeling back the clouds. William drove slowly back down the High Street, busy with bustling Friday shoppers, and parked his Mini at the back of the Nook.

The restaurant was open at midday with a limited menu for business lunches and light snacks, and although Marcia and Carl were perfectly capable of organising this session, either he or Leon always popped in to make sure everything was running smoothly.

William gave a snort. He couldn't remember the last time Dad had even bothered to put in an appearance at these lunchtime sessions. In fact, he couldn't remember the last time he himself had had a whole day off.

Things were going to have to change if he was to stay at the Nook.

'Hi, William.' Marcia grinned at him, pausing in the middle of setting the last of the tables. 'No problems. Everything under control. Seven tables booked, the rest ready for casuals, deliveries in and stored, no staffing problems. You can go home now!'

William returned her grin. Marcia was extremely efficient, and her husband, Carl, was quite able to manage the kitchen at lunchtimes. They had run their own restaurant in Dawley, had taken early retirement, then found that time hung heavily on their hands. They had been the day-time backbone of the Nook for five years now.

William pushed through to the apparently chaotic kitchen. One quick glance told him that everything was perfect. Carl and the three lunchtime waitresses were drinking coffee and he poured himself a cup from the percolator.

'Er — Lisa isn't working today? She hasn't phoned in?'

The girls shook their heads in unison.

'Leon coming in today?' Carl questioned. 'I really need to speak to him about the fishmonger . . . '

'Speak to me.' William drained his coffee cup. 'Dad probably won't be in until tonight.'

'William — ' Marcia poked her head round the door. 'You've got a visitor out front. She says she won't come through to the kitchen.'

William walked into the silent restaurant to find Lisa standing awkwardly just inside the door.

'Lisa!' He smiled at her, the smile dying as he drew closer. 'What's happened?' His lovely, laughing Lisa looked dishevelled, dirty and extremely tired. Instinctively he put his arms around her.

'Oh, William . . . I'm so sorry.'

'I've been so worried, Lisa. I went to

your bed-sit and — '

She stiffened in his arms. 'What did she tell you?'

'I wasn't prying.' William stroked her damp, unruly hair. 'But I do know you're moving out.'

'That's why I didn't come in to work. I know I should have phoned but I couldn't. I didn't know what to say.'

'It's all right,' he soothed her. 'It can't be that bad. Which of the dragon's rules did you break?'

'No children or pets ... ' Lisa muttered.

William shook his head, with the glimmer of a smile. 'So which of those cardinal sins did you commit?'

Lisa looked at him with huge sorrowful eyes. 'Both.'

★ ★ ★

Rosa had cleaned the dining-room until it gleamed. She changed all the beds, dusted the spare bedrooms, washed the kitchen floor ... and a glance at the

60

grandfather clock in the hall told her it was still only lunchtime.

She had been quite unable to relax, waking heavy-headed and feeling sick and remembering . . .

Throwing herself into a frenzy of housework seemed to be the only way to deal with the tight knot of fear that clamped in her stomach.

It need not be an affair . . . Maybe it was a casual thing, a one-off that he'd never meant to happen? Did that make it any better?

She swallowed the lump in her throat. One thing was certain — until Leon chose to come home, she wouldn't know . . .

She heard the key in the lock and called out, 'Leon? I'm in the dining-room . . . ' Her mouth was dry.

The door opened slowly and they stood facing each other.

'I . . . I slept at Steven's. We had a bit of a session. I — um — slept on the sofa. With the cats.'

Irrationally, she felt sorry for him.

There was none of his usual bluster.

'Really? That was after you left the Nook, was it?'

'Yes.' He walked to the window. 'Rosa, I'm sorry I didn't phone you. You might have been worried . . . '

'I might have been,' she agreed, amazed at the way her words could sound so calm when her whole life was falling apart. 'As it was, I slept like a log.'

'Good. You haven't been sleeping well lately.'

'You've noticed? Goodness me!'

'Please, can we talk, properly?' His face was etched with pain. 'About selling up, about the Four Seasons . . . about our future . . . '

'One of those subjects, yes.' She clenched her trembling hands together. 'Our future, Leon, if we have one. Who is she?'

He rocked back as though she had struck him. There was no need for him to say anything more. She knew this was serious.

'Do you love her?' It wasn't the question she'd meant to ask but it was the one that had been scalding her tongue since last night.

Leon's eyes searched hers, as if seeking an answer that wouldn't hurt. He had never been cruel.

'Yes.' He had never been a liar, either.

That was it then. The end of everything. You couldn't fight love . . .

She turned her head away.

'Rosa, look at me.'

'I'm not crying, Leon. And you didn't ask me how I knew . . . '

'Was it Steven?'

'Steven?' Anger flared again. 'You mean Steven knew?'

'Yes.' Leon sighed heavily. 'But he didn't approve. He told me to go home and patch things up.'

'Well, bully for him!' Her voice cracked like a whip. 'Dead simple for you men, isn't it? A bit of a dalliance, then run home with flowers and chocolates and say sorry and all will be forgiven!'

'No! That wasn't what I meant! Steven really is on your side — '

'Oh, I'm flattered! I didn't even know I had a side to be on until last night when she drove you home and kissed you goodnight . . . ' Her voice broke and Leon took a step towards her.

'Don't come near me! Is it for her that you're selling Cookery Nook and Honeysuckle House? It all seems a bit of a coincidence.'

'No, of course not. I want the Four Seasons for us. You and me and the children . . . '

'Priceless!' The tears were falling now. Angrily Rosa wiped them away.

'Listen to yourself, Leon! You've just told me you're in love with another woman but you still expect me to go ahead and support your stupid dreams!'

She took a deep breath. 'I will make an appointment to see Paul Beatty as soon as possible. I have no desire to rob you of anything that's yours, so I'll secure my side of the business and the house — and you and Miss World can open a burger bar in Acapulco for all I care!'

She swung round and tried to leave before the tears erupted again.

Ashen-faced, Leon reached out and gripped her arm.

'I still love you, Rosa. I can't lose you and the children.'

'You love us all, Leon.' Her voice was weary as she looked down at the familiar hand holding her arm. 'But that's not the way the game is played. Someone always gets hurt somewhere along the way. You had a choice, and that choice didn't involve me. Now, if you'll excuse me, I've got things to do.'

'Do you want me to leave?'

'Oh no, I'm not making it easy for you. That would be a great salve to your conscience, wouldn't it? You'd be able to tell everyone that I threw you out.

'You're my husband, Leon. I meant every word of my marriage vows. I remember the for better or worse part clearly — it's a shame you forgot about forsaking all others.'

Somehow she got out of the room. It was only when she reached the odd-shaped corner of the utility room, where the children had kept roller skates and tennis rackets and wellingtons and footballs over the years, that she allowed her grief to escape in shuddering sobs.

Half of her wanted him to leave because of his infidelity and his professed love for Her. The other half wanted him to stay because he was her husband — and because, despite everything, she still loved him.

'Mum? Why are you in the utility room?' Kizzy skidded to a halt. 'Oh, what's up? Have you got a cold?'

'I think so . . . ' Rosa sniffed, hastily wiping her eyes. 'Why have you come home?'

'It's lunchtime, and I thought I might catch Dad. I need to talk to him.'

'He's in the dining-room, Kizzy, but I wouldn't — '

But Kizzy had gone, her long red curls escaping from their combs, endless legs in black tights scampering across the tiled floor.

'Hi, Dad! Oh — have you got this cold, too? You look lousy. Never mind — I've got some news that'll cheer you up! Something for you and Mum to look forward to!'

⋆   ⋆   ⋆

Rosa walked along the shingle track, head down, aware of the afternoon sun warming the back of her neck and this morning's rain making iridescent patterns on the pebbles beneath her feet.

That was all she was aware of. Thoughts and plans, hopes and fears jumbled through her aching head, making no sense at all.

'Are you dashing off somewhere important or have you got time for a coffee?' Steven appeared in the doorway of his shop just as she passed. 'Rosa . . . ?'

'Don't waste time on tea and sympathy.' She raised her head and almost glared at the man she had always considered her friend. 'Or even coffee and sympathy. I know Leon stayed here last night and I know why. And I don't want to talk about it.'

'Ah . . . Right.' His smile faltered. 'I wasn't taking sides by allowing Leon to kip down with the cats. I did it because — ' He sighed. 'Well, because he's a friend and because he had nowhere else to go. I'd have done the same for you.'

'Thanks!' She gave a cynical laugh which faltered into a sob. 'Only I'm hardly likely to be intending to run away with a blonde in a flashy car, am I?'

'Rosa, please don't . . . ' Steven patted her shoulder awkwardly. 'I'll put the kettle on. Look, Leon said you knew nothing . . . '

'Oh, I knew nothing all right.' She gulped back the tears. 'Right up to the minute I watched him kiss her good-night . . . '

'I'll definitely put the kettle on.'

Steven disappeared into the shop. 'Take a seat, please. Don't run away . . . '

Run away, Rosa thought, lowering herself into one of the battered armchairs Steven kept at the shop to enable prospective purchasers to browse through the second-hand books in comfort. If only I could. But this pain could never be eased by avoidance.

'There.' Steven pulled up a chair opposite her. 'I've practically filled it with sugar. Oh, Rosa — I don't know what to say. But I'm always here if you need a shoulder to cry on.'

'Thanks.' The coffee scalded her numb lips. 'I feel such a fool! I should have known . . . I should have guessed. I mean, I've seen it happen to other people and I've never believed that the wife is always the last to know.

'And another thing — ' She raised fiercely tearful eyes. 'I always thought that if this unspeakable thing ever happened to me and Leon, then I'd scream and bawl like a fish-wife and throw him out of my life for ever.

'But, it isn't like that . . . ' Her voice tailed away to a whisper. 'I love him, Steven. I still love him . . . '

'Of course you do.' He stroked her hair like a father comforting a distressed child. 'And I could cheerfully throttle him!'

Rosa sipped at the syrupy-sweet coffee without tasting it.

'I wish I could be sure that what I'm going to do is the right thing — for me and the children. That's what's important now. If Leon leaves us — which I honestly believe he will — then it'll be up to me to keep Honeysuckle House and the kids on an even keel.'

She put down her cup. 'Thanks for listening — and I'm sorry I shouted.'

'Dear Rosa.' Steven rose to his feet, helping her from the depths of the armchair. 'In the circumstances I think you're entitled to do more than shout. Come down here and scream and throw things any time you want. And don't forget, I'm only a phone call away — day or night.'

'Bless you.' She grazed her lips against his cheek. 'You may regret making that offer . . . '

'Never,' Steven said softly, watching her walk proudly away towards Sea Road. 'Never in a million years . . . '

★   ★   ★

The sea danced with diamonds beneath the pale sun, but today its beauty failed to touch her. She had made an appointment to see Paul Beatty at the bank on Monday morning. That would give Leon and her the whole weekend to decide what they were going to do. Now there was only one more visit to make.

The bus was just pulling up at the stop. Quickening her pace, Rosa hurried towards it.

She arrived to find Dawley was teeming with shoppers and visitors. The noise and the bustle only served to irritate her further. There were couples everywhere — young couples in love, and older couples, contented, sure of each other. She swallowed the lump in her throat.

Suddenly she caught sight of a tousled head and a green sweatshirt, darting through the sea-front crowds.

'Jamie? Jamie!' She raised her hand and waved, but the boy didn't stop and was soon swallowed up in the scurrying mass.

She shook her head, feeling foolish. Of course it couldn't have been him. Jamie was at school in Highcliffe, not shoving his way round these infernally noisy arcades. Poor Jamie — how would he react to Leon leaving? And William? And Kizzy? Kizzy with her romantic dreams of perfect love. Kizzy — a real Daddy's girl . . .

She crossed the car park towards the office block of Brennan and Foulkes. Might as well get this over. There was no point in delaying any longer. There would be no sale of Honeysuckle House. No sale of her shares in

Cookery Nook. No Four Seasons being financed out of the only security she had.

'Do you have an appointment?' The pretty young receptionist smiled disarmingly.

'No.' Rosa shook her head. 'I'm sorry. I don't even know who I want to see. My name is Brodie. I believe my husband, Leon Brodie, has been dealing with one of your advisers. It's him I'd like to see.'

'Oh, yes!' The receptionist nodded with understanding. 'Mr Brodie. The Old Granary — Miss Phelps has been dealing with that account. If you'd like to take a seat, I'll make an appointment.'

'I'd rather like to see Miss Phelps now,' Rosa insisted. 'It's urgent.'

'I don't know . . . ' The girl looked at Rosa and her charming smile switched to a look of sympathy. 'I'll ring her and see what we can do . . . '

Nice girl, Rosa thought, staring at the abstract paintings in soothing sea shades that adorned the reception area. Efficient, too.

Idly, she wondered what Miss Phelps would be like.

'She's in Reception.' The girl was saying. 'No, it's urgent. A message from Mr Brodie. Sorry? Oh — no, she didn't ask for you by name. She didn't actually know who she wanted to see. All right, yes, thank you . . .'

She replaced the receiver, looking puzzled, then turned on her professional smile as she looked at Rosa.

'Miss Phelps is very busy, Mrs Brodie. She said if you could just leave a message she'll get back to you or Mr Brodie . . . Mrs Brodie?'

But Rosa wasn't listening. Beside the relaxing cool tones of the paintings was a who's who of Brennan and Foulkes; rows of sober-suited middle-aged male financiers and wheeler dealers — and one woman.

Beneath the picture of the beautiful blonde woman with the enigmatic smile were the words 'Felicity Phelps'.

And she knew who she was, all too well.

★   ★   ★

Slowly replacing the telephone receiver, Felicity closed her eyes. She couldn't pretend any longer. Rosa Brodie was no longer just 'Leon's wife', a hazy figure somewhere in the background, someone whom she had tried not to think about. Rosa Brodie was downstairs in Reception.

She walked shakily to the window overlooking the square, seeing nothing.

The Other Woman — was that what she was? A heartless husband-stealer caring nothing for Rosa or the children? She smiled faintly at the irony. If only that were true! It was because Leon was married that she had fought the feelings she felt for him for as long as she had. And now she loved him more than she had ever loved any man.

And his wife, the woman with all the rights, the woman who obviously didn't understand him, who seemed deter-mined to thwart his plans, was merely two floors below her.

Rosa Brodie had become a reality.

She picked up the phone. 'Nicky? Has Mrs Brodie left yet?'

'No, Miss Phelps.' Rosa opened the office door. 'Mrs Brodie hasn't . . . '

Letting the receiver drop back, Felicity faced the slender, brown-haired woman standing uncertainly in the doorway. When she'd allowed herself to think of Rosa she'd pictured her as a dowdy, middle-aged woman. This woman, with her casually-styled hair and jeans and sweatshirt showing off a trim figure, could, at first sight, have passed for Leon's daughter.

A wave of sickness swept over her, followed quickly by guilt. Trying to retain the ice-cool poise for which she was famed, Felicity took deep, steady-ing breaths.

Rosa was quite unprepared for Felicity's beauty. The fleeting glimpse in the moonlight and the harshly posed photograph downstairs certainly didn't do her justice.

Leon had always had an eye for a pretty face, she thought sadly. Like most men. But unlike most men, he hadn't been able to leave it at that . . .

'Mrs Brodie.' Felicity tried to calm the trembling. 'I'm so sorry — I did ask the receptionist to give you a message. I simply don't have time to — '

'I'm sure you don't.' Rosa surprised herself by speaking evenly. 'However, Miss Phelps, as you seem to have more than enough time for my husband — no, please don't deny it. I saw you last night when you dropped him outside our home.

'And, believe it or not, that isn't why I came here today. I didn't even know who you were . . . However, now I'm here, I'll kill two birds with one stone. May I sit down?'

'I really don't think . . . ' Felicity began, her composure shattered by Rosa's serenity.

'Well, I do.' Rosa sat in one of the

honey-coloured leather armchairs, wondering if Leon had sat here, smiling lovingly at this beautiful woman in the expensive suit the way he had once smiled at her.

'I came here to tell whoever was dealing with Leon's affairs — ' she paused and bit her lip ' — that as far as I'm concerned the Four Seasons is no more than a pipe-dream.

'Of course, now I know who you are, it puts a different light on things. However, please don't waste any more time in encouraging my husband to sell all that he has to finance a whim. I won't be selling my shares in Cookery Nook, nor will I agree to the sale of Honeysuckle House. If you and Leon are determined to buy the Old Granary for your country club, then I suggest you start looking for other means of finance.'

'I'm not entering into a business partnership with Mr Brodie.' Felicity felt as though the floor was moving beneath her feet. She struggled to regain some professional composure. 'At Brennan and Foulkes, we merely assemble business plans, find financial backing and set the wheels in motion. Leon — I mean, Mr Brodie — approached me on that basis. And I'm afraid I really am unable to discuss this any further . . . '

'Of course you are.' Rosa took a deep breath. 'I'm not a complete innocent in the ways of business, Miss Phelps. All I wish to make clear is that whatever plans you and my husband may have, they will not include taking away my security or that of my children.'

'Mrs Brodie — ' Felicity felt tears stinging her eyes. 'I didn't mean this to happen. Oh, I don't expect you to believe that but it's the truth. I'd — I'd feel better if you shouted . . . '

'Of course you would.' Rosa stood up slowly. 'So would Leon. But I rarely shout, Miss Phelps. And I certainly don't intend to start now, not even to make you feel better.'

She moved towards the door, aching

to turn and scream at this lovely woman to leave Leon alone and allow things to return to normal. But it was too late. Far too late. Nothing would ever be the same again.

She paused. 'I assume that you're in love with my husband, Miss Phelps? He has told me that he loves you. Leon is guileless. He's a charming dreamer — although you probably already know that. I've had to be the realist throughout our marriage — and apparently through its break-up. I do hope that you, too, can keep a grip on reality during the next few weeks because one of you will have to. Goodbye.'

Once the door had closed behind her, Rosa choked on the tears that she had been determined should not fall in front of Felicity Phelps. Stumbling down the staircase, feeling the nobbly plaster wall beneath her fingers, she prayed for numbness to return. There was a physical lump in her throat and a wrenching knot of pain in her stomach.

Felicity had not answered her question, nor had she needed to. Rosa had looked into those translucent green eyes and read the answer.

Felicity Phelps was hopelessly in love with her husband.

It's Time To Talk

Why haven't you got a ring then? How can you be getting married without even having an engagement ring?'

'Who're you having for bridesmaids?'

'Honestly, Kizzy, what did your mum and dad say?'

'Oh, Kizzy, you're so lucky! Andrew's just gorgeous . . . '

Surrounded by her friends, Kizzy basked in being the centre of attention. Her announcement had become the main topic of conversation in the Sixth Form common room, even eclipsing the horrors of the looming exams.

Her happiness fizzed inside her like a fountain of rainbows. She had no doubts at all. Doubts were for other people.

Who dared to say they were too young when she'd known for three years that she and Andrew were always going to be together?

She answered the questions with a beam. Of course she could always go to university later but her immediate future was to be working beside Andrew in his family's market garden and turning it into a garden centre. They had such ambitious dreams and nothing anyone said could take them away.

Miss Jenkins, the deputy head, frowned for a moment at the gaggle of giggling Sixth Formers, then smiled. She'd heard the gossip about Kizzy Brodie and had surprised herself by being secretly pleased for the girl.

Obeying her own parents' wishes, putting her career first, she had lost the only man she had ever loved, and now with a solitary retirement looming, she remembered only too well being young and in love and being loved in return. She still felt occasional pangs of regret in those lonely hours of waking just before dawn.

'I wouldn't have thought any of you

were so enamoured with school that you should still be lingering on the premises long after the bell has gone!' Miss Jenkins resumed her authoritarian role. 'Do you have no homes to go to?'

Quickly the knot disintegrated, still chattering like a flock of starlings.

'Kizzy.' Miss Jenkins raised her voice. 'May I have a word?'

Kizzy's heart sank. 'My revision timetable is up to date,' she began, 'and I've nearly finished the Chaucer essay and — '

'I have no doubts that it is and you have,' Miss Jenkins interrupted. 'You have always been a diligent pupil. Whatever plans you may have for the future, I know you'll make a success of them.'

Kizzy stared in surprise. Was this The Dragon's way of saying she agreed with her marriage plans? Who'd have thought it? If only she had Mum and Dad's support, too . . .

'No,' Miss Jenkins continued, 'I merely wanted to enquire about Jamie.

He had to be sent home after registration with another of those headaches and I wondered if he had seen the doctor?'

Kizzy thought quickly. Jamie had seemed fine at breakfast this morning, when they'd fought over who was going to do the washing-up. In the end neither of them had had time and they'd run out of the house in their usual last-minute hurry. He hadn't mentioned a headache. Not today or any other time.

'I don't know.' She looked down at her feet. 'I'll — er — find out over the weekend.'

'No doubt you have other things on your mind,' Miss Jenkins said drily. 'But Jamie is coming up to his GCSEs and he really can't afford to keep missing school. Perhaps I should speak to your parents about it?'

'No.' Kizzy answered quickly. She didn't know what exactly was going on at home, but she realised worrying over Jamie was something her parents wouldn't want just now. 'No, it's all right. I'll do it. I'm sure he'll be better by Monday.'

'Good,' Miss Jenkins nodded. 'Well, don't let me keep you . . . '

Swinging her bag over her shoulder, Kizzy wandered towards Sea Road. In five days Andrew would be home from Edinburgh and then they could make all the preparations. She'd ask Mum to come with her to Dawley to choose her wedding dress and Dad could sort out the Nook for the reception.

Andrew's parents had already started to clear out the chalet in the grounds of the market garden. Maybe she could ask Steven Casey to keep his eye open for some bits and pieces of furniture . . .

'Yes . . . over there, dear.' The voice of her mother's friend, Norma Beatty, floated over the hedge as Kizzy passed. 'No, not there! Honestly, Paul, you may be an excellent bank manager but as a gardener you're hopeless! You can't tell a weed from a willow! Give me Rosa any day.'

'Ah, Rosa.' Kizzy heard Paul Beatty sigh and involuntarily slowed her step. 'When did you last see her?'

'She called in yesterday, poor love. Leon's got some hare-brained scheme to sell the Nook and move to Dawley. I told her to let it ride its course. Look, put those cuttings over there . . .

'Leon's wonderful company and an amazing chef but I sometimes feel that he's never really grown up. I think if it wasn't for Rosa's practical streak they'd have gone under years ago . . . '

'Don't gossip, dear.' Paul straightened up with a groan. 'Oh, give me a dozen overdrafts to deal with rather than this gardening lark! Rosa's coming to see me on Monday. I wonder if it has anything to do with selling up?'

'Now who's gossiping?' Norma teased. 'But she told me Leon had been dealing with Brennan and Foulkes . . . '

'Then it's serious!' Paul whistled. 'Brennan and Foulkes don't take prisoners! I should have to advise very strongly about getting into their clutches. Dear, dear — I simply can't imagine Highcliffe without Rosa and Leon and the children . . . '

Kizzy stood like a statue. This couldn't be true! They couldn't be selling up and moving away without telling her! The bubbling happiness of only moments before evaporated into a cold blackness inside. She had to get home and find out the truth.

★   ★   ★

'You can't keep running away from it, that's for sure.' Steven Casey raised his head from the boot of his ancient car and looked at Leon. 'I think you've reached the point where choices have to be made, decisions taken. Here — make yourself useful. Take this lot inside for me.'

Leon took the armful of dusty books and chipped and dirty china.

'Just dump it anywhere out of sight.'

Steven closed the boot. 'I'll price it later. I'd offer you the job but it's nearly time for the evening session at the Nook, so no doubt you'll be donning your whites and creating some culinary masterpieces while I'm defrosting a pizza . . . '

'Not tonight,' Leon deposited the bric-à-brac in a discreet corner. 'William can run the restaurant tonight. I'm seeing Felicity . . . '

Steven shook his head as they made their way upstairs to the flat. 'Well, I suppose now Rosa knows who she is . . . '

'She doesn't,' Leon dropped on to the sofa beside the cats. 'But I'm sure she soon will. Oh, what a mess! If only Rosa had agreed to sell up we could have gone to the bank and I'd never have met Felicity . . . '

'So it's all Rosa's fault, is it?' Steven frowned. 'For goodness' sake, Leon! Look, I'm neither condoning nor condemning what's going on, but it's of your making. You can hardly blame

Rosa . . . Now where are you going?'

Leon had jerked to his feet. 'Home. I'll have to tell William I want him to work tonight, then try to talk to Rosa . . . '

'Tell her you're giving up Felicity and the whole crazy idea of the Four Seasons?' Steven fondled the cats. 'Is that it?'

'No, it isn't. I can't. I can't give up Felicity — and I won't give up on turning the Old Granary into the Four Seasons.'

'So instead you'll go on hurting Rosa and the kids.'

'Don't.' Leon shook his head. 'I thought you were my friend . . . '

'I am.' Steven's voice was weary. 'But I'm Rosa's friend, too. Look, Leon, I do understand how you feel about Felicity. These things happen. But don't you think you really ought to move out, even if it's just temporarily? Give Rosa some space — and you, too . . . '

As soon as he'd uttered the words,

Steven wished he could retract them. What demon had snatched at his tongue?

'I don't mean move in with Felicity or anything,' he added quickly. 'There's always my sofa.'

Leon clutched at the offer like a drowning man. 'You're a pal. I'll talk it over with Rosa. Now.'

That was the answer, Leon thought, driving his car along Steven's shingle road. If he moved out of Honeysuckle House it wouldn't be like finally leaving Rosa. His whole being jibbed at the thought of that. But it would make things so much easier. He could come to a decision without prejudice.

The High Street was busy with early evening traffic, and Leon filtered into it carefully. He felt happier now. Rosa would understand, and agree, he was sure. After all, their arguments were getting them nowhere.

And tonight he'd tell Felicity. He smiled. The thought of Felicity made him feel like a teenager again. He'd forgotten what a heady business love was . . .

'Mum's having a bath and Dad's not home yet,' Jamie announced from the depths of the sofa as Kizzy glowered in the doorway. 'What's so important, anyway?' He pulled a face. 'Has Andrew cancelled the wedding? I knew he'd see sense!'

'It's nothing to do with the wedding! My wedding is the only normal thing that's happening to this family.'

'Normal? Huh!' Jamie sniggered. 'It'll be like something out of 'The Munsters'.'

'Brat!' Kizzy hissed. 'And if you knew what I know, you wouldn't be laughing. How much longer is Mum going to be?'

'Hours, I expect.' Jamie turned back to the television. 'You know what women are like. All that fussing over their hair and make-up and trying to make themselves beautiful when it's all a waste of time.' He grinned cheekily at his sister.

Kizzy slid down on to the sofa and pinched her brother hard. 'Listen, clever-clogs, I want you to clear out of the way when Dad comes home, OK? There are things I've got to talk to them about. In private.'

'I'm watching telly.'

'Well, you can watch it in your room!' Kizzy snatched at a cushion and hit him hard.

'Ow! Watch my head.'

'That reminds me.' She narrowed her eyes. 'How's your headache?'

Jamie wrinkled his nose. 'What headache?'

'Precisely. The Dragon was really worried. Said you'd had to go home again. She said she was going to talk to Mum and Dad . . . '

'She didn't?' Jamie's face was ashen. 'She hasn't, has she?'

'Not yet, but I'm sure she will.' Kizzy gazed at him appraisingly. 'So what have you been up to? Cutting school, that much is obvious. But why?'

'None of your business.' Jamie still looked frightened. 'Anyway, why should you care? You've got your precious Andrew and your soppy wedding. William's got the Nook. Mum and Dad don't listen to anything . . . What do any of you care?' He jumped to his feet.

'Jamie — ' Jamie was on the verge of tears, and despite their spats, Kizzy loved her brother dearly. 'What is it? What have you been up to? Can I help?'

'No!' Jamie swallowed, his lips trembling treacherously. 'No-one can help! I'll be in school on Monday — and if you mention any of this to Mum and Dad, I'll kill you!'

'Jamie, wait!' Kizzy raced from the sitting-room in pursuit of her brother, but he'd thundered up the stairs and into his bedroom.

Leon unlocked the front door just as Kizzy reached the hall. 'Hold on — where's the fire?'

'What? Oh, that was Jamie. We — er, we were having an argument. Dad, we've got to talk.'

Leon was shaking his head and laughing. 'You and Jamie, still fighting — you'll never grow up! Where's your mother?'

'In the bath. Dad, tell me it's not true!'

Leon had wanted to talk to Rosa alone, but there was no gainsaying Kizzy's baleful glare. He looked at his pretty, flame-haired daughter.

'Tell you what's not true?'

'That you're selling the Nook and the house and moving to Dawley. It's not true, Dad, is it?'

Leon suddenly felt icy cold. Taking a deep breath, he reached out to take Kizzy's hands in his.

'Say something!' she implored him. 'Tell me what's going on.'

'Yes, why don't you do just that . . . ' Neither had noticed Rosa emerging from the bathroom. She reached the foot of the stairs, her dressing-gown cord trailing behind her, her hair wrapped in a towel. 'Don't you think

Kizzy is owed an explanation, Leon?'

'Then it is true!' Kizzy's eyes filled with tears as she gazed at both her parents. 'You were going to do it without even telling me — or William or Jamie! You can't! You just can't!'

'Come through to the sitting-room.' Leon still held her hand. 'We'll talk in there.' He looked at Rosa. 'Won't we, darling?'

'Don't, Leon,' Rosa's voice was no more than a whisper. 'Not that.' She turned to Kizzy and smiled shakily. 'Dad's right — and so are you. We do need to talk.'

Leon and Kizzy sat on the sofa while Rosa perched on the chair opposite them.

'So, what have you heard? And more to the point, who from?' Leon asked.

Ashamed to admit that she'd been eavesdropping, and terrified by her parents' lack of denial, Kizzy twisted tendrils of hair tightly round her fingers.

'It doesn't matter where I heard it,

does it? What matters is that other people know what's going on in this family before I do. Why are you selling?'

'We're not,' Rosa leaned forward, casting a quick glance at Leon, willing him to support her. 'It's not as straightforward as that. There may be changes in the future, but nothing's decided yet. Kizzy, love, we'd never make any major changes without telling you — any of you.'

'But there is something going on, isn't there?' Kizzy was still frightened and angry. 'Are we bankrupt or something?'

'Nothing like that, but as your mother says, there may be some changes in the future.' Leon squeezed his daughter's hand. 'And yes, they may — just may — involve selling up the Nook and maybe moving out of this house to an even nicer one at Dawley. But I promise you that when we decide what we're doing, we'll involve you all in the discussions. All you need to do is concentrate on your exams, Kizzy, and not listen to gossip.'

'Why not?' Kizzy jerked her hand from her father's grasp and jumped to her feet. 'I don't believe you! Jamie's right — you don't care about anything any more! Well, I won't be moving out of Highcliffe! When Andrew and I are married, we're going to live in the chalet and I don't care if you decide to move to the moon!'

'Kizzy, don't.' Rosa's own heart ached at her daughter's anguish. 'And we really must wait until Andrew comes home before we say any more about this wedding. I thought I'd made it clear that we both — ' Again she shot a look at Leon. ' — want you to consider waiting.'

'Never!' Kizzy's face flamed almost as red as her tumbling curls. 'You can't stop me! I'm eighteen, and as soon as I've taken my A-levels I'm going to marry Andrew whether you like it or not! Why should I wait when you're planning to move away? I'm not going to let you ruin my one chance of being happy. I'm not going to let you ruin my life even if you want to ruin your own!'

She ran from the room, across the tiled hall and up the stairs, and a door banged distantly.

Rosa had jumped to her feet, half angry at Kizzy's rudeness, half understanding the pain behind it.

'Let her go,' Leon said quietly. 'She's had her say, and she's very on edge with her exams coming up and her head filled with this wedding nonsense.'

Rosa sank back into her chair. 'Maybe, but now she'll go barging into Jamie and give him some garbled version, which will have been further embellished by the time it reaches William. Leon, we're going to have to be honest with them soon.'

She swallowed the irritating, constant lump in her throat. 'Honest, Leon. Do you remember honesty?'

'I remember a lot of things,' he said quietly. 'Including times when we knew exactly what to say to each other, as well as our children.'

Trembling, Rosa interrupted him. 'I suppose the amazing Felicity Phelps would have handled it with kid gloves.'

Leon's eyes widened in disbelief. 'How — who told you?'

'She did.' Rosa was again aware of the strange calm acceptance washing through her body. 'This afternoon. When I visited Brennan and Foulkes.'

'You did what?' Leon had jumped to his feet. 'What on earth possessed you to go there? What did you say to her?'

'You'll have to ask her.' Rosa also stood up. 'And meeting the gorgeous Miss Phelps was not intentional, I assure you. I had no idea who she was until I got there.' She sighed. 'But our very enlightening conversation has led me to one conclusion, Leon. This situation has to be resolved. And now. You can see what it's doing to Kizzy — you're not being fair to the children.'

Leon's silence spoke volumes and Rosa stared at him. With his hair flopping forward across his forehead, his eyes still seemingly kind and caring, he could easily have been the crazy young catering student she had fallen in love with. She wanted to cry.

Leon moved his hands towards her then dropped them with a futile shrug. She was his wife and yet he could offer her no comfort. Rosa didn't want his guilty caresses. She wanted all his love. And that was impossible now.

'Where are you going?' He watched as she tugged the towel from her hair. 'Rosa, stay and talk. There are things I need to say.'

'They'll have to wait a little longer,' Rosa rubbed at her hair. 'I need some fresh air to clear my head. I need some space.'

'So do I,' Leon muttered to himself in the desolate twilight silence. 'So do I . . . '

★   ★   ★

The air of suspended reality took control again as Rosa walked slowly away from the early evening bustle of the High Street. It was the sort of inner strength she'd discovered after the death of her parents in a car crash when she was just nineteen.

Leon loved Felicity Phelps; Felicity Phelps loved Leon equally.

That left Rosa with three children and Honeysuckle House; with a share of the income from Cookery Nook, and no skills to offer the outside world save those of housewife, mother, and gardener.

'Face it,' she spoke aloud. 'Before long you're going to have to take responsibility for bringing money into the home, and who on earth is going to employ you? So, Rosa Brodie, just what are you going to do?'

'Bad habit, that.' Steven paused in removing the display of books from outside his shop. 'I do it all the time — and all my habits are bad!'

'What?' Startled, she peered into the mauve dusk, unaware that she'd even been walking in the direction of Steven's place.

'You're talking to yourself.' Steven grinned at her. 'Personally I always find it helps a lot. Have you seen Leon?'

'Why?' She traced patterns on the shingle with the toe of her shoe. 'Has he been here?'

'Earlier. He said he was going home to talk to you.'

'That would be a novelty.' Rosa looked up and met Steven's eyes. 'Yes, he did. Or at least he tried. Kizzy had heard rumours and gave us the third degree — and then I confronted him with the information that I'd spent the afternoon with Miss Phelps.'

'You what?' Steven's eyes widened.

Despite her weariness, Rosa smiled. 'Oh yes, I know who she is now. And she's — she's very lovely . . . Oh, Steven!' Tears welled in her eyes and fell heavily on to her cheeks, and she dashed them away with her hand, angry at her vulnerability.

'Rosa . . . ' Steven slid his arm round her shaking shoulders. 'Oh, I feel so useless! Come inside and talk about it.'

★ ★ ★

Rosa sat on the sofa with the cats on her lap, her tears mopped by Steven's large hankie, a mug of coffee liberally laced with brandy clenched in her hand.

Steven listened attentively as she told her story.

' . . . so, that's it,' she finished. 'That's how it happened. I think I behaved quite well. In other circumstances I'd probably even have liked her! And at least it solved one problem.'

'And what's that?' Steven placed his own coffee on the table and turned down the Mozart on the stereo to a gentle hum.

'I made up my mind that when Leon leaves me for her — which he will, so don't make any fatuous remarks — I'm not going to be the bereft little woman sitting at home existing on hand-outs and sympathy. I'm going to survive. And I'm going to survive so well that

Leon will wonder what on earth he left me for. I'm going to go into business myself and out-superwoman Miss Perfect!'

'Good for you,' Steven dropped down beside her. 'And what exactly do you intend to do? Become the next Richard Branson?'

'I haven't a clue!' Rosa's laugh lodged in her throat, emerging as a groan. 'Why are you looking at me like that? I mean it . . . '

'I know you do.' He leaned closer. 'And that's why I'm looking. You're an amazing lady, Rosa. I know you'll succeed and emerge from this mess bloodied but unbowed. Does Leon really know what he's losing?'

Suddenly his face was close to hers, his gentle eyes asking unspoken questions. Rosa stared at this man who had been her friend for as long as she could remember and knew that he was going to kiss her.

For a moment she stiffened, almost recoiled, then as his warm lips sought hers, she gave herself up to the sweetness.

For twenty-four years she had kissed no-one but Leon — and Leon had never kissed her like this. The warmth, the love, the need in Steven's kiss found an answering echo in the depths of her lonely, frightened body. With a shuddering sigh, she felt herself responding, and amidst the warmth and the blissful soaring music, Rosa returned Steven's kiss with a passion long-forgotten.

Steven's True Feelings

The silence roared around them, broken only by the rhythmic purring of Steven's two cats. Shocked and embarrassed, Rosa stumbled to her feet.

'Rosa.' Steven's voice was unsteady. 'Don't go. I'm sorry, I didn't mean to . . . Don't walk out now.'

'I'm not.' Rosa couldn't look at him. 'I — I was going to put some more music on . . . or something . . . '

'At least that's more original than offering to make a cup of tea,' he said, sounding a little more normal. 'Rosa, look at me.'

She turned, a pile of CDs in her hand, her freshly-washed hair tumbling across her flaming cheeks. 'It was just — just silly,' she said shakily. 'I was feeling so low . . . I should have stopped you.'

'No you shouldn't.' He got to his

feet. 'It was something that we both needed. Anyway, what's a kiss between friends?' He smiled tenderly at her.

'Steven, that was not a friendly kiss . . . '

'Well, it wasn't unfriendly, was it? Here, what do you fancy?' He took the CDs from her trembling fingers. 'Gershwin? Vivaldi?'

'No, nothing. Oh, I don't know . . . ' She looked into his eyes. 'Steven, that must never, ever, happen again. I'm no better than Leon . . . '

'Don't ever say that!' Angrily he pushed the Gershwin into the player. 'What he's done to you is unspeakable. Think about it, Rosa — if he hadn't got entangled with Felicity you wouldn't be here alone with me. Nothing would have happened. So don't blame yourself. You're a lovely lady who deserves to be treated a whole lot better than Leon has ever treated you.'

'That's no excuse for throwing myself at you.' Rosa blushed at the memory. When Steven laughed, she flared up.

'It's no laughing matter! We're not children! We should know better.'

Steven held up his hands. 'I'm not laughing at you. Listen to me, Rosa. You didn't throw yourself. You were sad and vulnerable — and I've wanted to kiss you like that for longer than I can remember.'

Rosa shook her head slowly. 'But you're Leon's friend — and mine. And you've had hundreds of glamorous girlfriends. Norma Beatty and William both told me you were in the Nook with a new one only this week.'

Steven reached out and took her hands in his. 'And why do you think that is? Why do you think I still play the field? What if I told you it was all because the only woman I could ever imagine spending my life with is married to my best friend?'

'Oh no!' This time she managed to free her hands. 'No, Steven! You don't mean that! You're only being kind to me because of Leon.'

'No.' Steven shook his head, his eyes

gentle. 'I'm not being kind, Rosa. Selfish, insensitive, timing things badly — and explaining them even more so — yes. But kind, no. What I'm being is honest.'

Downstairs, the shop bell jangled loudly, and Steven sighed impatiently, then smiled again. 'See what you've done — it's the first time I've ever not wanted a customer! Look, pour a couple of drinks. I won't be a second.'

'I ought to be getting back. I must talk to Leon tonight . . . '

'Yes, of course. But don't go until I'm sure you're OK. Just stay and have a drink first, then I'll run you home. It's getting dark — I don't want you walking home on your own.'

There were far more things to be frightened of than a walk home in the dark, Rosa thought. Things like losing the man you loved to someone younger, prettier, better educated; things like alienating your children; things like facing a future that held nothing.

Things like being kissed by a man

whom you'd only ever thought of as a friend — and enjoying it so much that your heart raced like a teenager's at the memory . . .

'This must be some sort of family reunion.' Steven's voice echoed with false gaiety from the other side of the door. 'Rosa was just leaving.'

He opened the door and, with an imploring glance at Rosa, ushered Leon into the room.

Confronted by her husband, she felt a red-hot surge of pain and anger. 'There's no need to follow me around.' She winced at the biting tone of her own voice. 'I said I was going for a walk. I'm not suicidal.'

'I didn't know you were here.' Leon seemed edgy. 'I left you a note . . . '

'Why? I was just coming home.'

'Because I had a phone call from the Nook. William hasn't turned up and no-one has heard from him. They've got a full restaurant and no chef!'

'Well . . . I'll be down in the shop if anyone wants me,' Steven said, discreetly backing out of the door.

Neither Leon nor Rosa said anything until he closed the door, then they both spoke together.

'Rosa, what we were saying about making a decision — '

'Leon, we really must talk — '

They stopped, irritated.

'Go on.' Leon ran his fingers through his hair. 'You first.'

'I was going to say — ' Rosa stopped in mid-sentence, her eyes moving down to floor level. 'What's that?'

'My suitcase — and a few bits and pieces.' Leon swallowed, feeling tears gathering behind his eyes. 'I — I'm moving in with Steven for a while. He suggested that I stay here while we sort things out. Face it, Rosa, we're getting nowhere.'

He paused, and when he spoke again his voice was racked with emotion.

'Can — can you tell the children that I won't be coming home . . . ?'

★   ★   ★

'Shouldn't you be at the Nook?' Lisa turned anxious brown eyes towards the wall clock. 'They've been open for nearly an hour.'

'Dad's responsibility.' William shrugged. 'I can't remember the last time I had a night off. He hasn't been in that kitchen for more than half an hour for weeks. This is far more important.'

Lisa gave him a grateful smile and resumed wrapping her scant possessions in sheets of newspaper. William, on his knees beside her, was careful not to appear too protective. Lisa was fiercely independent.

Goodness knows what it had cost her finally to tell him the truth. The two nights she'd spent in bed and breakfast to escape her landlady here must have been truly awful.

Even here, the drabness of her living conditions brought a lump to his throat. She had tried so hard to turn the austere room into a cosy home, with cheap table lamps to cast a warm glow, bright cushions on the threadbare bed-settee, postcards framed for pictures on the dingy walls. Yet nothing could really detract from its cold anonymity.

A sharp rap on the door made them pause in the middle of their packing.

'Yes? Who is it?'

'Mrs Evans.' The landlady's voice echoed through the thin door.

Lisa scrambled to her feet and opened the door. Immediately, the middle-aged woman whom William had seen earlier in the day jabbed an irate finger in his direction.

'No men in the rooms, Miss Ross! You know the rules!'

'I'm helping her pack.' William sat back. 'Not moving in.'

'And don't be giving me any cheek, neither!' Mrs Evans' face turned an unbecoming red. 'She's broken all the other rules of the house — *my* house — so I suppose it was only a matter of time before she sneaked a man in!'

'He's my employer.' Lisa gnawed at her lower lip. 'He's not stopping. I'm just moving my stuff out.'

'Good job, too! And don't you ask for no refund on your rent, young lady! I was within my rights to throw you out the minute I found out what you were up to!'

William stood up and towered above the landlady.

'As I understand it, all Lisa was trying to do was provide a home for herself.'

'Herself and her child — not to mention that crazy dog! In one room! In my house! I let rooms to single business people, professionals, not unmarried mothers with wild animals! And what's your interest? Are you the father of that baby? Because if you are, I think you ought to know that she's an unfit mother!' She stabbed a finger at Lisa. 'Dragging it out till all hours of the night. Leaving it alone with goodness knows who!'

'Get out!' William roared. 'Close that door and go downstairs and mind your own business! As you seem so keen on spouting rules and regulations, may I remind you of tenancy rights? Lisa has paid for this room and you are violating her right to privacy!'

Mrs Evans stepped forward, then thought better of it. Without another word, she turned and left the room, and William slammed the door behind her with such force that the entire house quivered.

'Wonderful!' Lisa's eyes were glistening with tears of laughter. 'It's what I've been longing to do to her for months! How on earth did you know all that stuff about tenancy agreements?'

'I made it up.' William grinned. 'I haven't a clue! But then, neither has she, obviously.' He stroked tendrils of dark hair away from Lisa's cheeks. 'Why on earth did you come to live here with someone like her?'

'I told you. It was cheap and I was desperate.' Lisa looked away from him. 'There aren't many places that will take children and animals, and I had nowhere else to go. I had to lie. There was Lewis — and I've had Otis since he was a puppy.'

She turned back to him, her eyes beseeching. 'William, that wasn't true, about me being an unfit mother. I do look after Lewis in the best way I can. It's not my fault I have to work late hours. The woman who minds him for me is young, but she has her own kids and she doesn't charge much . . . '

William picked up her slender hand. 'If only you'd said something.'

Lisa shrugged slightly. 'Ever since Lewis was born, I've met with opposition. By the time I'd got to know you properly, to like you, it was too late.' She gulped. 'I couldn't tell you then. I — I didn't think you'd be interested in me if you knew I had a six-month-old son.'

Hauling her to her feet, William handed her the last of the cardboard boxes.

'Let's finish packing and get out of here. And you don't know me very well or you would never have made that last remark. It came as a shock, I'll admit, but it doesn't alter you, does it? Or the way I feel about you . . . '

With everything stowed in the Mini and the keys returned to Mrs Evans, William drove away from the tall houses that edged the Common.

'Do you want to go straight back to the bed and breakfast place now?'

'Not really.' Lisa shook her head in the darkness. 'But I'll have to. Could we pick Lewis up on the way? And I ought to pop in and see Otis at the animal sanctuary. They'll only board him free of charge for a week.'

'Otis first then.' William turned out of the High Street. 'I can't wait to meet this wild animal that terrified Mrs Evans!'

'He's as soft as butter!' Lisa giggled. 'A big, shaggy baby. He was usually fine on his own.' She sighed. 'If he hadn't howled that night, Mrs Evans would never have known about him — nor gone into the room and seen Lewis's pram . . . '

'Thank goodness he did, then,' William said with feeling. 'At least it got you out of there. But where will you go after this week? Back home?'

'Out of the question, I'm afraid.' Lisa's voice was almost lost beneath the noise of the engine. 'That's why I'm in this mess. My parents were horrified when I told them I was expecting a baby. I'd known they would be, of course, but I'd hoped they'd understand.'

She turned her head away and looked out across Highcliffe's darkness. 'They didn't. We lived in a small village and their attitudes were pretty rigid. I — I went away to have Lewis and I've never been back.'

'Don't they want to see their grandson?' William was shocked. He could understand Lisa's parents being angry and disappointed, but surely they couldn't turn their backs on their daughter and her child?

He was sure that if it had been Kizzy, Mum and Dad would have been fighting over who was going to change the next nappy or mix the next feed, once the dust had settled.

'And what about Lewis's father?' he asked tentatively. 'Didn't he want to marry you?'

'No!' Lisa's voice was angry. 'And don't ask any more! I can't tell you! There are things about me that you'll never understand.'

'OK.' William reached across and patted her hunched shoulders. He could take his time — Lisa had told him more tonight than in the whole four months he had known her. 'But what I do understand is that by this time next week you and Lewis and Otis will be homeless again.'

He smiled in the darkness of the car. 'And I think I may just have the answer to that . . . '

★   ★   ★

'Are you sure you'll be OK?' Steven looked worriedly across at Rosa in the

120

car's cosy darkness as they pulled up outside Honeysuckle House.

'I'll be fine,' Rosa assured him. 'And at least now I won't lie awake just waiting . . . At least now I'll know that he's not coming home.' Her voice quavered. 'This is the break we both needed, Steven. We knew it had to come. Now I can start to sort out my life.'

He gently touched her cheek in a gesture of support and friendship. He knew as well as she did that her brave words had no substance.

'Of course. And I meant what I said about phoning me. Any time, Rosa. Promise me?'

'I promise. Although Leon may answer the phone when I do . . . '

'So?' Steven stroked her cheek again, thinking that Leon would spend far more of his new-found freedom in Felicity's luxury apartment than sharing his lumpy sofa with the cats. 'I've always been friends with you both.

'Do you want me to come in with you?'

'No thanks,' she said quickly. 'Steven, if you mean that — that you're my friend — please don't say anything to spoil it. I need friends now, not complications.' She turned to face him. 'You're a wonderful man — but Leon is still my husband. He's still the man I love . . .'

'And the man you love has just left you to tell his children that he's not coming home!' he retorted angrily. 'How much longer will you cover up for him, Rosa? How many more excuses will you make?'

'Stop it!' Tears stung her eyes. 'This is our marriage — our problem. No-one in the world knows Leon like I do. Not even you! Certainly not Felicity Phelps.'

'Oh, Rosa.' Steven sighed. 'You don't deserve this.'

'No sympathy!' Rosa choked back the tears. 'You'll only make me cry again. I'll ring you in the morning. Thank you — for everything.'

'You're more than welcome.' He reached over and brushed her lips with his own. 'There. A kiss between friends.'

'And that's how it will have to stay,' she said wistfully as she slid from the car. 'Goodnight, Steven.'

Waiting until she had closed the front door behind her, Steven started the car and drove thoughtfully back to his flat — and Leon. He laughed at the irony.

Rosa closed the door and leaned against it, at last allowing the private tears to fall unchecked. Tonight, the house seemed large and empty. Tonight and all the other nights, because Leon, with his laughter and his bluster and his mercurial moods, had gone.

★   ★   ★

Upstairs, Jamie heard the door close and moved away from his bedroom window, his thoughts racing. Kizzy had told him that they might have to sell up

123

and now he knew why. Mum was having an affair with Steven Casey!

He jabbed at his eyes with an anguished movement. He remembered Robert Walker in his class last year. His mum had left his dad. The other boys had laughed at him when they'd caught him crying in the changing rooms . . .

Jamie swallowed. He hated everybody! His mum. Kizzy. But most of all he hated Steven Casey! Pulling the duvet over his face he cried until his throat ached and his head was swimming.

Leaving her own room, Kizzy heard the muffled noise and paused outside her brother's door, her hand on the latch. Then, thinking better of it, she moved away and padded downstairs to the sitting-room.

'Mum? Why are you sitting in the dark? I couldn't concentrate on my revision. I rang Andrew. He said I should apologise to you.'

She switched on the light and looked

in horror at Rosa's puffy face and unchecked tears. 'Oh, Mum! What's happened?'

Rosa scrubbed at her eyes, blew her nose and held out her arms to Kizzy. She held her daughter closely, trying to regain some control of her emotions.

'What Dad and I told you earlier, about selling the house and the Nook, wasn't strictly the truth, Kizzy. We won't be moving away from Highcliffe — not from this house, nor from the Nook. But Dad will. He's — he's left, Kizzy.'

'What do you mean, left?' The girl's voice was high with panic.

'I mean that your father has moved out.' Rosa stroked her daughter's glorious hair. 'He's staying with Steven for a while. Things — things haven't been right for ages and — oh, there are lots of reasons. But we both felt that we needed breathing space.'

'But you can't separate! Other people's parents separate — not you and Dad! You've always laughed and been happy together.'

'Long ago, Kizzy, if you think about it. A very long time. Dad isn't happy. It's nothing to do with you or the boys — he just isn't happy.'

'Is he — ?' Kizzy shook her head in disbelief. 'Is there someone else?'

Rosa said nothing, just cuddled Kizzy against her as she had when she was a baby, drawing comfort from her closeness.

'There is!' Kizzy was crying now. 'Oh, how could he? How could he?'

They cried together then, mother and daughter. Rosa had no thoughts, only a numbing blackness in her head, but Kizzy's brain was reeling.

As the only girl, she knew that she had a special place in her father's heart and she idolised him in return. It was because of him she'd been so sure about Andrew. Andrew reminded her of Leon. Honest, open, good-natured, a gentle man with a head full of dreams . . .

'Who?' She croaked the word. 'Do I know her?'

'No.' Rosa wiped her daughter's tears. 'No, you don't. And neither did I until today. She's young and beautiful and clever — and she's encouraging your father to sell up and open some leisure complex in Dawley. That's how they met.

'Look, Kizzy, there are two sides, always. I've no doubt his will sound different.'

'I'll never listen to his side!' Kizzy sat up, scraping her hair away from her damp face. 'If he can turn his back on you — on us — then he can stay away for ever. But don't worry, Mum. I'll look after you . . . '

Rosa looked on in surprise as Kizzy uncurled herself from the sofa and padded towards the kitchen. 'Where are you going?'

'I'm going to make some hot chocolate and find that spiced rum and make two hot-water bottles and then we're going to bed.' Kizzy tried to make her voice sound normal but it was difficult when her heart was breaking. 'And no arguing.'

★ ★ ★

Kizzy sipped her hot chocolate, curled on her parents' bed. Only it wasn't any more, she reminded herself — it was Mum's. Treacherous thoughts started to steal into her mind, of long-ago Christmas mornings when she and William and Jamie had staggered into this room, weighed down by pillow-cases bulging with exciting parcels. There had been so much laughter and happiness.

Determinedly she slid her feet to the floor and pattered to the window where Rosa was staring out over the blackness.

'Even the sea is angry.' She turned to Kizzy. 'Thanks for the drink and the hot-water bottle, love. It helps . . . '

'I know.' Kizzy squeezed her mother's arm. 'It's what you used to do for me, remember? Remember when I had that stupid crush on Ben Taylor? And then he asked Stephanie to go to the pictures? I thought my life was over! But you gave me a hot-water bottle and chocolate and a cuddle and told me that one day I wouldn't even remember what he looked like.'

'And you think it will be that easy with Dad, do you?' Rosa smiled sadly.

'Of course not.' Kizzy shook her head. 'But then, it's not the same thing, is it? Dad will come back to you.'

Maybe, Rosa thought, hugging the hot-water bottle, but will I want him back? Am I strong enough to forgive him for this? Even supposing he does tire of Felicity, do I love him enough to be able to rebuild our marriage?

'What are you going to tell Jamie?' Kizzy broke into her thoughts.

'The truth.' Rosa sighed. 'He's old enough to understand. But there's no way I want any of you taking my side against your father's. You'll still see him — he'll still be welcome here.'

'Not by me he won't!' Kizzy asserted.

'Jamie and William must do what they want. Boys see things differently. We women feel the pain.'

We women. Rosa looked at her daughter with new eyes. Kizzy had grown up in a few short hours. Not once had she complained about Leon's defection ruining her life, her plans. Her thoughts and sympathies had been all for Rosa.

'Kizzy,' she began. 'I'm very proud of you . . .'

'Don't be silly.' Kizzy hugged Rosa. 'You're my mum and my best friend. You'll find out you've got loads of friends. Everyone loves you.'

Steven? Rosa thought suddenly. Did Steven love her, too? Was that what he was telling her? Maybe it was like Kizzy and Ben and Stephanie all those years ago. Everyone loving the wrong person.

Jamie was thinking of Steven, too, but not with love. He listened to the rise and fall of the voices from Rosa's bedroom with increasing anger. Stupid Kizzy with her head full of soppy weddings. Always reading love stories and crying at soft films on TV. She would think Mum and Steven kissing and cuddling was OK. She wouldn't give a thought to Dad!

But if Dad wasn't going to be around any more, then neither was he. Pulling on jeans and sweatshirt, and sliding his feet into his trainers, he opened his bedroom door.

Rosa and Kizzy, lost in their own world, heard nothing as Jamie pulled open the front door, shivered slightly in the blustering gust from the sea, then stepped outside into the darkness.

Nowhere To Turn

'I'm so sorry about last night.' Leon stood up and took Felicity's hands in his. 'I really did want to see you.'

'I missed you, too.' Felicity smiled, kissing his cheek. 'But these things happen — and at least you phoned. Didn't William show up at all?'

'Not a word from him.' Leon waited until she had sat down before resuming his own seat. 'I was up to my eyes in brochette of monkfish and linguini until midnight!'

'Sounds fascinating.' Felicity laughed. 'And after midnight?'

'I crashed out on Steven's sofa. It's for the best. Rosa understands . . .'

'Maybe.' Felicity sighed deeply. 'But I still feel guilty, I can't help it.'

'Do you want me to go back to her?' Leon stared into the big green eyes. 'If so, just say, 'it was nice while it lasted

132

but you're a married man and I'm not prepared to wreck your marriage'.'

'That's not fair!' Felicity turned her head away from him. 'You know I can't end this any more than you can.'

They were silent for a moment, sharing the turbulent emotions of love and guilt.

The quayside café at Dawley was practically empty at this time of day, the early-morning shoppers just beginning to arrive at the car park, and the late holidaymakers still enjoying their breakfasts in numerous establishments along the sea front.

'Full English breakfast?' Leon asked over the top of the menu. 'Or continental?'

'Just coffee and rolls.' Felicity smiled again. 'I can never eat first thing.'

'I can.' Leon caught the waitress's eye. 'Especially at weekends. Rosa always does a full fry-up.'

'Good,' Felicity said tersely. 'Cooking is not my forté, as you well know, so that's one thing your wife and I don't have in common. Don't expect break-fasts liberally drenched in cholesterol from me.'

'Is that an invitation?'

'No, just a warning.'

They were smiling at each other again, and the tension had passed.

Leon watched Felicity as he was aware all the other men in the café were watching her. She was stunningly attractive — and all the more so because she was unaware of it. Yet it wasn't her looks he was in love with. Had it been that shallow, maybe extricating himself would have been easy.

No, Leon admitted to himself, he loved Felicity Phelps because she was the other half of him. Whatever Steven said and Rosa thought, this was no last-ditch grab at his youth. This was the love he had wanted all his life. A love that he had never expected to find and certainly hadn't looked for.

He'd loved Rosa — he still did — but not in this way.

Unselfconsciously they held hands across the table as they sipped their coffee, watching the growing bustle along the quayside through the café windows and making plans for the rest of their day.

Opposite the café, the amusement arcade was already screaming with garish life. Leon watched the youngsters crowding through its gaudy portals and wondered sadly how his own children had reacted when Rosa had told them the news. He'd go round tonight and make sure they were OK, that they understood. He knew they would. It wasn't as if they were babies.

And he was only at Steven's — he threw a glance at Felicity and was warmed by her smile — at least for just now . . .

★ ★ ★

Shivering despite the sun, Jamie stood in the doorway of the arcade, his back to the road, drawn by the lights and the noise. The spectrum of brilliant colours offered sanctuary and oblivion. The machines with their rhythmic music, their hypnotic flashing illuminations, their perpetual promise, lured him like sirens. He stepped inside, unable to resist.

He had almost ten pounds in his pocket. A fortune. Enough to feed the machines for ages. What else was there to do? He certainly wasn't going home — not with Mum and Mr Casey behaving like Kizzy and Andrew. And he couldn't find Dad until the Nook opened . . .

As he fed his first coin into the slot, his fingers itching to punch out the sequence that spelled success, he wondered if they'd missed him yet.

He was good at these games. Better than most. Here was something he excelled at. Something he could be proud of. He'd become something of an expert and a lot of people stopped to watch him as his fingers worked with the same rapidity as his brain.

Lulled by the repetitive sound and motion, he let his mind wander. He wondered if Mr and Mrs Beatty would find out that he'd slept in their summerhouse last night. When he'd beaten this machine he might ring them. He might tell Norma Beatty about Mum and Steven. Then she'd let him stay with her. Mrs Beatty was kind and she loved him, Jamie was sure of that. So did Dad.

Brilliant! He'd done it! People were clapping and patting him on the back. This was happiness. He'd tell Dad when he went to the Nook . . .

Then he turned — and saw them. They came out of the café, their arms round each other, laughing. He'd seen them together before. His dad and that blonde woman who looked like a film star.

He felt violently sick. The shivering started again. The noise and the lights and the arcade seemed very far away.

They didn't see him. Jamie watched his father and the stranger as they crossed the road towards the town centre, still laughing.

Slowly he stepped outside, not knowing where to go next. He couldn't go home. Home meant Mum and Dad — and they didn't even want each other . . .

Norma Beatty? He thought longingly of the cosiness of the Beattys' large shabby house and the comfort of Mrs Beatty's plump arms, then shook his head. The Beattys were in Highcliffe and Highcliffe was home. He was never going home again . . .

His fingers closed around the ten-pound note folded in his pocket. It crinkled reassuringly. Shoving his hands deep into the pockets of his jeans, he wandered towards the sea-front. It was still early. Mum wouldn't even know he hadn't been at home last night. He wondered what she'd say when she opened his bedroom door.

The sea was sprinkled with white foam flecks, and there were already people on the sand; people walking with dogs and children. Families.

Jamie leaned his elbows on the rails, his eyes skimming the scene. Angrily he scuffed at the scattered sand beneath his trainers, telling himself it was the sea spray making his eyes sting and his throat ache.

Blinking hard, he turned his concentration to a big black dog darting in and out of the waves, chasing seagulls, barking at the breakers. Even dogs have families, he thought, watching the tall, blond-haired man calling to the dog, and the girl with the dark hair blowing about her face pushing a pram bumpily towards him, laughing. Everybody laughing . . .

'William!' In his surprise, Jamie said the name out loud. He couldn't believe it. What was his brother doing here?

'Jamie?' William squinted towards the promenade. Then louder, 'Jamie!'

Jamie had turned, started to run. William, with his longer legs and faster stride, tore across the beach and up the uneven steps two at a time. He had to find out why Jamie was in Dawley this early. And, more importantly, why his little brother was running away from him.

With a final sprint, he stretched out his hand and grabbed Jamie's shoulder.

'Let me go!' Jamie squirmed in his brother's grasp. 'Leave me alone! You can't make me go back!'

'What are you talking about?' William panted, tightening his grip. 'What's going on?'

'You know!' Jamie shouted. 'You know! And you probably think it's all right! But I don't!' His temper fragmented into tears and he lashed out again.

'Hey!' William side-stepped his brother's flailing arms and legs. 'Jamie, what on earth is the matter?'

'Ask them!' Jamie yelled through his tears. 'Ask Mum and Dad! Just let me go!'

Aware that a little crowd had gathered, William gritted his teeth. 'Steady, Jamie, just calm down.'

His quiet tone had its effect and Jamie stopped kicking.

'Now, tell me — what's happened with Mum and Dad?'

Hanging on to Otis's collar, Lisa brought the pram to a halt beside them.

'Who's she?' Jamie glared at William. 'You're just the same as them! Secrets! Everyone's keeping secrets!'

'I — I work at the Nook.' Lisa looked at Jamie with sympathy. 'Are you Jamie?'

He turned angrily on William. 'See! She knows about me but I don't know anything about her!'

Wriggling again, he broke free and stood still for a moment, his face contorted. 'Mum is going out with Steven Casey!' he spat through white lips. 'And Dad's got a girlfriend! And you've got her!' He jabbed a trembling finger at Lisa. 'I hate you! All of you!'

This time William wasn't quick enough to stop him as he ducked away along the promenade. He sped after him, calling: 'Jamie! Jamie!' But his voice was caught by the mocking wind and tossed back to him.

Finally, out of breath, he panted to a halt. The boy had run towards the town centre, and he'd lost him in the twisting maze of streets and alleys.

He shook his head. What on earth had Jamie been talking about? Mum and Steven? Dad and another woman? It couldn't be true. He'd have known, wouldn't he? Or had he been too wrapped up in his own affairs to give more than a passing thought to the problems at home?

'William?' Lisa reached him again, having bulldozed her way along the crowded promenade with the pram and Otis. 'What's going on?'

'I wish I knew!' He ran his fingers through his hair. 'The poor kid is obviously frantic about something! All that rubbish about Mum and Dad. Goodness knows where he's hared off to now! We've got to find him.'

'Poor Jamie.' Lisa bit her lip. 'Look, I'll go that way through the precinct

142

and you take the back road across the Market Square. We'll meet up here in about half an hour.' She paused and grinned. 'What a way to begin my introduction to your family!'

'You'd better get used to it.' William managed to smile. 'Lewis will be a teenager one day and — '

'William!' Lisa grabbed his arm. 'Look!'

They stared in disbelief as a London express coach moved slowly past them. Jamie, ashen-faced, was slumped in the back seat.

* * *

'I'm not so sure the spiced rum was a good idea.' Rosa winced as she unloaded the washing-machine. 'I think I've got a hangover.'

'It served its purpose, though.' Kizzy paused in making two mugs of coffee. 'You slept all night.'

'It was lovely, honestly.' Rosa straightened up and looked gratefully at

143

her daughter. 'Being tucked up in bed with the hot-water bottle, listening to the wind and drifting off feeling all warm without a care in the world.' She sighed. 'It's a pity it was all still there when I woke up . . . '

'Positive thinking,' Kizzy admonished sternly, placing the two mugs on the scrubbed kitchen table. 'That's what we decided last night.'

Rosa's smile didn't reach her eyes. 'We've still got to tell the boys.'

'Oh, let them sleep a bit longer.' Kizzy stretched lazily. 'Jamie was upset anyway and goodness knows what time William came in. I didn't hear him.'

'Neither did I, but you're right. He could certainly do with a lie-in. He's been working far too hard.' Rosa sat down, nursing her coffee. 'I'll tell them separately. William first, then he can be there to cushion Jamie.

'Oh, I could throttle your father! Has he any idea what he's done?'

'Probably not.' Kizzy bit her lip. 'But he will. Then he'll come running back and everything will be all right, even if — ' She paused, hearing a key in the lock. 'It's him! I don't want to talk to him, Mum, not yet!'

She jumped from her seat just as William walked into the room.

'Oh!' Kizzy stared at her brother. 'I thought it was — I mean, why aren't you upstairs?'

'I've been out,' William snapped, his eyes resting on Rosa. 'Mum, what's going on here? We've just seen Jamie — '

'Jamie?' Rosa tried to clear her muzzy head. 'Where? And who's 'we'?'

'Mum, listen to me. I saw Jamie in Dawley this morning. Why was he fighting me? And why is he going to London?'

Rosa rubbed her hands across her eyes. 'What are you talking about? Jamie's upstairs in bed.'

'He certainly isn't.' William ran his fingers through his hair. 'He's on the express bus to London!'

Feeling cold fingers of panic grip her

throat, Rosa gazed at William, only dimly aware of Kizzy racing upstairs to check her brother's bedroom.

'I was in Dawley,' William said quickly. 'I saw Jamie and he tried to run away. When I caught him he was crying and he told me — well, that doesn't matter right now. Anyway, he was frantic about something. He said some very weird things. He managed to give me the slip and the next thing I knew he was on the London bus.'

Slowly Rosa shook her head. 'We'll have to contact the police, get them to stop the bus before it reaches London.'

Kizzy returned white-faced to the kitchen. 'He's gone. What are we going to do now?'

'I'll phone the police.' Rosa jumped up. 'Tell them what's happened. Get them to have a policeman meet the bus at Victoria . . . ' She clenched and unclenched her hands. 'Jamie's never been to London in his life! He's got no money! He — '

William placed firm hands on her

shoulders. 'Calm down, Mum. I'll phone the local police station, explain that he's run away, give them a description. Don't worry, he'll come back . . . ' He paused. Jamie had been so distraught. And London was no place for a fourteen-year-old alone. 'We'll find him.'

'I'll ring the police,' Kizzy said quickly, realising that Rosa was close to collapse. 'You stay here with Mum, William.'

★   ★   ★

Listening to Kizzy's young, confident voice on the phone, Rosa sank down at the kitchen table. 'What exactly did Jamie say?'

'That you — 'William stopped. 'That you're going out with Steven Casey. That Dad has got a girlfriend. That he hates everyone . . . '

Rosa sighed. 'Your father left home last night. This isn't how I'd planned to tell you. And I didn't tell Jamie

147

— goodness knows how he found out . . . ' Her voice wavered. 'But I'm definitely not having an affair with anybody.'

'But Dad is?' William's voice was ragged with disbelief. 'He's left you? For someone else?'

'Yes. She's a partner in Brennan and Foulkes. He met her when he wanted financial advice.'

William had walked to the kitchen window. The sea sparkled, sprinkled with diamonds. The sky was blue.

He should have known.

He turned to face his mother. 'So where did Jamie get this business about you and Steven from?'

'Goodness knows!' Rosa felt a surge of anger. 'Maybe he couldn't believe that Leon was the guilty party — you know how he worships him. Maybe he wanted to make it my fault.'

Kizzy came back into the kitchen. 'The police are sending someone round. They'll try to get an officer in London to intercept him when he gets off the coach. They'll want a photo and details of what he was wearing. They said not to worry . . . '

'Huh!' Rosa pushed back her chair. 'Of course I'll worry! It's all my fault — I should have explained things to him last night.'

'We'll explain things to him when he comes home,' William assured her with a confidence he didn't feel. 'The important thing is to get him back.

'Kizzy, put the kettle on, will you? I'll be back in a moment.'

He hurried out of the house and down the drive. Otis, practically filling the back seat of the Mini, barked a frantic greeting as Lisa wound down the window. 'Is there anything I can do?'

'I don't think so.' William slid into the front seat of the car beside her. 'I think I'll have to drive up to London and fetch the little blighter back. Mum doesn't drive. And Dad has left home . . . ' His words hung in mid-air.

'Oh, William.' Lisa reached for his

hand. 'I can't believe it! Your dad always seems so happy when I see him at the Nook.'

'I don't think it was Mum who was making him happy, though,' William muttered. 'Oh — blast him! Why did he have to do this? Mum looks like she's dead on her feet, Kizzy's behaving like a maiden aunt, and Jamie's on his way to London! I hope Dad's proud of himself!'

'I'd be better out of the way,' Lisa said quietly. 'I'll take Otis back to the animal sanctuary and go back to the bed and breakfast. I'll ring you tonight.'

'No!' William turned to her and buried his face in her thick dark hair. 'You'll never be in the way. I want you to stay. More than ever now.'

He gave a half-smile. 'You can stop at the house with Kizzy while I take Mum to London. You'll have to get to know the rest of the family sooner or later, although I'd have preferred it not to be in these circumstances.'

He scrambled from the car again,

lifting the carrycot from the back and grabbing Otis's collar. 'I love you, Lisa, remember that. So — are you ready to meet the family?'

'Are you sure this is a good idea? Don't you think your mother has enough problems? Maybe we should leave it until Jamie's home and things are more settled with your dad . . . '

'I don't think there's ever going to be a good time. Look, you can't stay at that bed and breakfast place any longer. Please come in — really, you'll be doing me a favour. I don't want to leave Kizzy on her own while I tear off to London . . . '

★   ★   ★

Rosa wandered round Steven's shop, picking things up, looking at them and putting them down distractedly.

' . . . so I left them with Kizzy cooing over the baby and the dog eating chocolate biscuits on the patio. Oh, why hasn't William come back! It shouldn't take him this long to find Leon.'

'Leon may not be at Felicity's.' Steven shook his head. 'William won't waste any more time than is necessary looking for him. Look, I'll give Leon a message — you can ring here as soon as you reach London.'

'Oh, this is a nightmare!' Rosa rubbed her eyes. 'This morning I thought — I really thought that now Leon had moved out, and once the children knew, life would return to some sort of normality. That I could face up to things and move on. And now this happens . . . '

'It's life.' Steven moved across the shop, between the second-hand furniture and piles of books, and looked down at her. 'Life has a habit of not running smoothly. So, the police think it's a good idea for you to go to London, do they?'

'Sergeant Delaney said it was probably the only way. He was very kind. He says the London police will stop Jamie when he gets off the coach and hang on to him until we get there. Kizzy and Lisa are going to stay at home in case Jamie comes back or phones.' She swallowed painfully. 'Oh, Steven — he will be all right, won't he?'

'Yes, of course.' Steven drew her against him, almost afraid to touch her, but knowing that she desperately needed comfort and reassurance. 'Are you sure you don't want me to drive you to London?'

'I'd love you to. But if Jamie thinks that Leon left home because you and I were — you know . . . No, I don't think it would be a good idea.'

'No, probably not. I wonder what on earth made him think of it?'

'Goodness knows!' Her sigh was muffled against the musky warmth of his sweater. 'I don't think I know any of my children any more. Kizzy has behaved like an angel, when I was expecting tantrums and condemnation. Jamie has taken off to London. And William . . . ' She sucked in her breath. 'William presents me with this pretty girl, a baby, and a huge lollopy dog, all of whom seem to form a major part of his life, and expects me to welcome them with open arms when I had no idea of their existence!'

'But, despite being frantic about Jamie, devastated by Leon, and completely at sea generally, you welcomed them all with your smile and told them to treat Honeysuckle House as their home?'

'Well — yes,' she admitted. 'How did you know?'

'Because I know you, Rosa Brodie.' He tightened his arms about her. 'You've got the biggest heart in the world.'

'All the more to get broken,' she retorted, drawing away from him as she realised just how much she was enjoying being in his arms. 'Oh — listen!'

The Mini screeched to a halt outside, scattering shingle.

'Any luck?' Steven called from the doorway.

'No.' William shook his head. 'I went to the address you gave me for this Felicity Phelps, but there was no reply. Then I went to Brennan and Foulkes's office, but it was all closed up. I even drove out to the Old Granary, but there's no sign of him.'

'I'll keep trying,' Steven said tersely. 'I've got Felicity's number. You get your mum up to London and find Jamie. I'll look after things here.'

'Thanks.' William grinned. 'I'd be grateful if you could check on Kizzy and Lisa, too — and tell Carl and Marcia they'll probably have to run the Nook tonight. We've got a silver wedding party booked in.'

'Leave it to me.' Steven opened the passenger door for Rosa. 'You just drive safely — I'll take care of this end.'

Rosa flashed a grateful smile at him as the Mini roared away across the shingle. William glanced at her curiously. 'He's a great bloke.'

'Yes.' Her voice was soft. 'I know . . . '

★ ★ ★

The road to London was heavy with traffic so that they seemed to take ages. Rosa's stomach twisted itself in a knot of foreboding as awful images flashed through her mind. Suppose they were too late? Where would they start looking? And when night fell, what would Jamie do then?

'Um . . . Lisa seems a nice girl.' She turned to William, trying to take her mind from Jamie's plight. 'I hope I'll see more of her — in happier circumstances. Goodness knows what she must think of us.'

'Lisa understands.' William threaded his way carefully through the traffic. 'She's had several knocks of her own. She certainly isn't going to stand in judgment.'

'And the baby? He's gorgeous. Is — is she married?'

'No.' He cautiously overtook a swaying caravan. 'I don't know anything about her background. I met her at the Nook.'

Rosa closed her eyes. The Nook. So much part of her life, and yet for months she had known nothing of what went on there.

'Oh? Was she a regular customer?'

'She's a waitress.' He grinned. 'And if you want to know any more you'll have to ask her.'

'I'm not prying — ' she began hotly, then she caught the glint in his eye. 'Stop teasing me. It's natural for me to be curious. I'm your mother.'

William smiled, greatly relieved that, for a while at least, the trauma over Jamie seemed to have slipped to the back of her mind.

Rosa looked at her son. How like Leon he was! Charming, funny, teasing. If only it were Leon driving; if only things were different and she and Leon were heading up to London to see a show, or, more usually, to snoop round someone else's restaurant.

William turned off the motorway. 'Nearly there.'

Victoria Coach Station was buzzing

with Saturday arrivals and departures. They hurried to the main office and soon a kindly official with a clipboard was leading them towards a uniformed policeman.

'Mrs Brodie.' The officer turned to Rosa. 'Your son — or at least, a boy answering his description — did board the coach at Dawley. Unfortunately he wasn't on board when the coach reached Victoria. The coach made two stops before this one. We can only assume that he got off at one of those.'

* * *

The Nook was crowded, but not full. The silver wedding party was in full swing, and the waiting staff seemed to be coping admirably.

'I'm not stopping,' Leon began apologetically as he walked into the kitchen. 'I just need a quick word with William.'

'He's not here.' Carl stared at Leon in surprise. 'Marcia and I had a call from Steven Casey saying neither you nor William would be in tonight. Some sort of family crisis, he said.'

'What crisis?' Leon frowned.

'I've no idea. But surely you've seen them today?'

'No — er — I've been out all day.' Leon began to feel stirrings of panic. 'I'll ring Rosa and find out. Thanks for standing in tonight . . . '

'No problem.' Carl shrugged as Leon reached for the phone.

The phone was answered as soon as it rang.

'Kizzy? What's wrong? Where's your mother?' He paused, listening, the colour draining from his face. 'I'm on my way.'

Slamming the phone down, he tore from the kitchen with no explanation, only adding to the speculation already bubbling amongst his staff.

The lights from the house blazed across the front garden as he pulled into the drive. He'd never forgive himself if anything had happened to

Jamie. How could he have thought that leaving Rosa for Felicity would be calmly accepted by his children? Had love made him so naive? But while he'd spent the day with Felicity, walking in the sunshine along Dawley's cliffs, holding hands, laughing at nothing and everything, Jamie had run away.

As the front door opened, Leon was suddenly aware of a throaty growl and a volley of barking. A huge black dog hurled itself on him, licking his face and his hands, its tail whirling like a rotor blade.

Lisa appeared and grabbed Otis. 'Sorry, Mr Brodie,' but her words were drowned out by a sudden squall from Lewis, wakened by the commotion.

Leon glanced towards the sitting-room.

'My son.' Lisa was scarlet with embarrassment.

'Dad!' Kizzy appeared in the kitchen doorway.

Leon looked at his white-faced daughter and his heart ached. What had he done to his family? 'Kizzy, what's going on?'

'We'll talk in the dining-room,' Kizzy said, sounding remote and cold.

Leon followed his daughter, feeling as though he'd walked into some nightmare where normality evaded him. Dazed, he sat down at the table.

'Kizzy, can you just please tell me what's going on?'

'Like you told me?' She faced her father across the table. 'Like you told us all about your girlfriend and how you couldn't bear to be with us a moment longer? Like you told us how you had to walk out on Mum to be with someone else?'

'Kizzy — ' Leon reached out to his daughter. 'I know how you feel. And I should have told you. It's just . . . there wasn't a right time. Just tell me — what's happened to Jamie? Where's Mum? And William?'

'London.' Kizzy swallowed, knowing her voice was trembling, trying to be strong. 'Jamie caught a bus to London, to get away from all this — Mum and William have gone up there to find him.'

A knot of fear tightened in Leon's heart. 'Where in London?'

'Victoria. That's where the bus was going. But he could be anywhere. He's fourteen and alone in London, thanks to you. You make me sick, Dad! Don't you know you belong here, with Mum?'

'I — Kizzy, your mother understands — '

'Understands that you love someone else more than her?' She tugged at the tendrils of hair round her face. 'And how do you think that makes her feel? She'll take you back, Dad! She'll forgive you.'

Leon could feel the tears pricking the back of his eyes. 'Kizzy, marriages end. People fall out of love. But I'll never stop loving you, darling . . . '

'Don't you dare talk to me about love! Don't you dare talk to me about anything. Just go up to London and bring Mum and Jamie back . . . '

She turned away, her slender shoulders shaking, and Leon moved to hold her as she sobbed. How often in her life had he comforted her like this? Once she had welcomed his comfort. Now he felt her fighting against it.

'I love you, Kizzy,' he muttered against her hair. 'You're my daughter. My only daughter. You've always been special to me. Darling, don't cry. Please don't cry. It'll be all right . . . '

She tried to push him away. 'Leave me alone. Go and find Jamie . . . '

'And when I do, we'll talk.' He turned her tear-stained face to look at him. 'Promise me, Kizzy? When I come back, we'll talk?'

She said nothing, and reluctantly Leon let her go.

'Will you be all right on your own?'

'Yes. Lisa's here.' She sniffed. 'She's staying the night.'

'I didn't know you knew each other.'

'We didn't. She's William's girlfriend. I thought you'd have known that — but

I suppose you've had other things on your mind.'

'Kizzy.' Leon's eyes searched her tear-stained face. 'Please, don't judge me until we've had time to talk. Please.'

'Go and find Jamie,' Kizzy repeated, but this time there was a softening in her blazing eyes. 'I think that's the most important thing right now.'

Leon leaned down and kissed her cheek, and with a surge of relief realised that she hadn't flinched away from him.

It was a start, he thought, as he drove away from Highcliffe. If he could just make Kizzy understand . . .

William would discuss it man to man. He didn't think William would take sides. And Jamie? Once he realised that his parents' separation didn't mean that Leon would be permanently out of his life, surely he'd be all right? But Kizzy, his only daughter. He couldn't risk losing her . . .

Second Thoughts?

Leon unlocked the door to Felicity's flat and stepped into the cool cream and white hallway.

'Where have you been?' She stepped from the bedroom, her hair falling in a glossy curtain to her shoulders, her midnight blue dress accentuating her perfect figure. 'You'll have to get a move on if we're going to make the theatre on time.'

'Felicity, I'm sorry, I can't go.' He caught her hands in his. 'Jamie has run away. Gone to London. I've got to see Sergeant Delaney at Highcliffe and then get up there.' He tried to pull her towards him. 'I'm sorry — '

'Stop saying sorry!'

'We can make the theatre another night. Felicity, he's only a kid. Rosa and William have already gone . . . '

'We can't make the theatre another

night.' Her voice was icy. 'The play leaves for the West End next week. Surely if Rosa and William are in London, they don't need you as well?'

'Of course they do!' Leon protested. 'He's my son, Felicity.'

'And Rosa is your wife. The wife you've left. For me. Because you love me. You've left them. Do you really think you can just go back? I'm quite sure Rosa and William will be able to cope without you.' She turned her face away, and her voice was hard.

Shocked at the bitterness in her tone, Leon moved to take her in his arms.

'Felicity, you don't mean that.'

'Yes. Yes, I do.' She turned her head so that her face was hidden behind the curtain of her hair.

'Felicity, please see this my way — '

'No!' She jerked her head up and Leon was amazed to see the big green eyes filled with tears. 'You see it my way, Leon. How do you think I feel? No sooner have you left Rosa, cast aside your past for our future, than you're running to her. The first time something goes wrong with your family — *your* family, Leon, not mine — then our plans fly out the window! I know leaving wasn't something you did lightly. But the decision was yours — I didn't force you. I just don't know where I stand . . . '

'Oh, Felicity.' He sighed. 'I'm so used to you being strong. I didn't think that — '

'You didn't think at all.' She sniffed. 'And neither did I. Oh, Leon, I'm jealous! I'm frightened. Frightened of losing you to your wife . . . '

He gazed at her steadily. 'Felicity, darling — I love you. For your strength — and now for your vulnerability. But I honestly don't have any choice. I have to go to London for Jamie's sake. Surely you can see that?'

Reaching for a hankie, she nodded. 'I know. I'm sorry — I'm over-reacting. I don't know how it feels to have a child. You do, so does Rosa. It's something you'll always share. Whatever happens in the lives of your children will pull you and Rosa together and I shall be left outside . . . '

She gave him a wan smile. 'Don't listen to me, Leon. Go and find Jamie. I'll still be here when you get back.'

'You'd better be.' Leon held her to him. 'I'll make this up to you, darling, I promise you. Anything you want . . . anything at all . . . '

Felicity watched the tail-lights of Leon's car until they were out of sight.

'Anything . . . '

A smile tugged at the corners of her full mouth. If he knew what she wanted more than anything in the world, he'd never believe it.

* * *

Leon drove away from the police station in Highcliffe, his thoughts see-sawing painfully between Felicity and Jamie. This was only the beginning. How many more times would his loyalties be divided? No, he thought, never divided — shared.

Following Sergeant Delaney's instructions, he headed for the police station in Victoria where they were co-ordinating the search, and where Rosa and William would be waiting for him.

Poor Rosa. She'd had far too much to cope with in far too short a time, and it was all his fault.

'I'm Leon Brodie.' He spoke to the policeman on the desk. 'My son, Jamie . . . I understand that my wife is here? Is there any news?'

'If you'd like to take a seat, Mr Brodie.' The policeman's voice was sympathetic. 'I'll get someone to take you through to your wife and let you know what's happening.'

Leon perched on a hard bench, but almost immediately a brisk policewoman approached him. 'Mr Brodie? If you'd like to follow me.'

'My son?' Leon asked. 'Have you found my son?'

'Sergeant Donaldson will talk to you in a moment.' The policewoman smiled, opening the door. 'Your wife and elder son are in here.'

William and Rosa looked up expectantly as the door opened, and Leon had never felt more awkward.

'I got here as soon as I could. What's happening? Have they found him?'

'Oh, yes.' William answered coldly. 'About half an hour ago. In an amusement arcade in Soho.'

'Thank God! And they're bringing him here?'

'Yes.' Rosa spoke at last. 'So you've had a wasted journey. Sorry to have spoiled your evening.'

'You haven't . . . Rosa, I know what you must have gone through.'

'No, you don't, Leon. You weren't here to go through it with us. But then, you're never around when anything matters, are you?'

*   *   *

'Lewis is sleeping soundly,' Kizzy whispered as she tip-toed back into the sitting-room and flopped down on to the sofa beside Lisa. 'And Otis is lying beside the carry-cot like a guardian lion.'

'He always does.' Lisa leaned over and refilled Kizzy's wine glass. 'They're inseparable.'

'Like you and William?' Kizzy teased, noticing Lisa's blushing face.

'You don't mind?'

'Mind? I'm delighted. William's thrown all his energy into the Nook for as long as I can remember. It's about time he had a girlfriend.' 'Yes, but . . . ' Lisa stared into her wine glass. 'I mean, there's Lewis.'

'Who is the most gorgeous baby in the world — and is no-one's business except yours.'

Kizzy curled her long legs beneath her with a sigh. 'Oh — this feels like the longest night on record. Still, it's a relief to know that Jamie's OK, though I wouldn't want to be in his shoes when they reunite him with Mum and Dad.'

'I suppose Mr Brodie will have reached there by now,' Lisa said, 'although when William phoned he said it was just him and your mum. Will they all come back here tonight?'

'Goodness knows.' Kizzy shrugged. 'I don't know what's wrong with Dad. Maybe he'll realise tonight that his family is more important than this woman.'

'I feel sorry for him,' Lisa murmured. 'I know it's tragic when a marriage ends, but he took me on when I was desperate, and I only ever saw him as a kind, big-hearted man. Whoever the other woman is, I — I can't blame her for loving him.'

Kizzy bit back her reply. Of course, it was different for Lisa.

'I don't know. I'm too close to see it that way. I just know how hurt Mum is. And Jamie. And I took everything for granted — this house, the Nook, my parents, being happy. I thought that was how things would always be!'

Lisa nodded in understanding. 'I know. I lost everything because of Lewis. But things do work out, Kizzy. You've got to have faith. Because of what happened to me, I met William — and now your family — and there's hope ahead. A few short months ago there was nothing.'

'And Lewis's father?'

'I won't talk about him. My life and Lewis's has nothing to do with him. Is that the front door? Surely they can't be back already?'

'No.' Kizzy got to her feet. 'More likely Steven, or Carl and Marcia from the Nook. Goodness — listen to Otis!' The volley of barking echoed through the house, closely followed by Lewis's wails.

'No peace for the wicked.' Lisa jumped up.

Kizzy padded across the tiled hall, shivering slightly after the snug warmth of the sitting-room, and pulled open the front door.

'Andrew!' She threw herself into his

173

arms. 'But you weren't coming home today! I can't believe it. Tell me I'm not dreaming!'

'You're not dreaming.' Andrew cradled her tenderly against him. 'Although I think I might be! How long have you had a dog and a baby?'

'Oh, they belong to William — sort of. Come on in . . . '

She dragged him into the sitting-room, not wanting to let go of him ever again, and surveyed him. Tall, stocky, with a tousle of shaggy dark hair and eyes like melted chocolate. Kizzy thought he was the most handsome man in the world.

'I've missed you so much. But why are you home?'

'The course work was over and I didn't think there was any point in hanging around. I missed you a bit, too, you know,' he teased. 'And after you'd told me about your parents, nothing could have made me stay in Edinburgh a minute longer than I had to. I've been driving for hours.'

'You mean you haven't been home yet?'

'No, I came straight here. Where are your mum and dad?'

'London — rescuing Jamie. I'll explain later.'

'So they're back together in London?'

'No. They're in London together, but separately, if you see what I mean.'

Andrew laughed, drawing her towards him and burying his face in the flowing cascade of her hair. 'Oh, Kizzy. This is what I've dreamed of, just this, and getting married. Being together for ever . . .'

'Me, too.' Kizzy mumbled fervently against his sweater. But even as she said the words, she felt a buzz of panic. Together for ever . . . That was what her parents must have thought . . .

'There are so many things to do now I'm home,' Andrew continued. 'How are Mum and Dad getting on with renovating the chalet? They've been sending me progress reports but I can't wait to see it for myself. It was a great idea of yours to ask Steven Casey to look out for some bits and pieces — we can make a really cosy little home.'

He looked down at her lovingly. 'All you have to do is concentrate on your A-levels. I'll take care of everything else.'

Again Kizzy smiled but deep inside she felt a stirring of unease.

Lisa appeared in the doorway. 'Oh, sorry! I didn't realise . . . '

'This is Andrew — my fiancé.' Kizzy moved away from him slightly, but still held his hand. 'Andrew, this is Lisa Ross, William's girlfriend. She's keeping me company while the rest of the family are in London.'

'Pleased to meet you.' Andrew extended his free hand, his eyes quizzical. 'Have we met before? You look familiar.'

'No. No — I don't think so.' Lisa looked quickly away. 'I've only been in Highcliffe since the beginning of the year. I met William when I started work at the Nook.'

Lisa turned to Kizzy, her eyes troubled. 'Would you mind if I went to bed? Lewis is settled again for now, but it'll only be a few hours before he's up again.'

'Of course.' Kizzy nodded. 'I've left a spare nightie and everything in the room for you. Sleep well — and thanks for being here.'

'It's been great,' Lisa answered with feeling. 'Oh, I know the circumstances were terrible, but to have a bedroom and a bathroom . . . ' She sighed. 'I'd almost forgotten the luxury. 'Night then.'

Once she'd gone Kizzy returned to Andrew's arms. 'She's been living in a really grotty bedsit — and now she's in bed and breakfast.'

'Poor girl. And the baby and the dog?'

'All of them apparently — and I don't know any more. William has kept very quiet about her. And she certainly doesn't want to talk about her past.

'Now, would you like some coffee?

Something to eat?'

'Both! And another kiss . . . And then maybe you can tell me just what's been happening here.'

* * *

Jamie slumped in the back of the police car beside the policewoman and watched the lights of London swirl past in the darkness.

This was like some nightmare that he couldn't wake up from. He was glad they were taking him back to Mum and Dad — the policewoman had assured him that both his parents would be at the police station to meet him — even if it did mean he was in for a major telling-off.

London had frightened him. He'd never admit it, of course, but the noise and the lights and the crowds that had seemed exciting when he'd first got off the bus had become intimidating. And he'd run out of money.

'You're not being arrested,' the

policewoman reassured him. 'Just rescued.'

If only they could make everything else all right. Make Mum and Dad be happy together again.

'Nearly there.' The woman looked down at him kindly. She liked this sad, tousle-haired boy, and was glad that, at least this time, the story had a happy ending. 'Are you hungry?'

'Starving. I had some chips ages ago.'

Jamie couldn't remember exactly when. It seemed like three days ago that he'd left the sanctuary of home.

'I expect we'll find you something in the canteen,' she continued kindly. 'We'll get that sorted first, shall we — before we see your mum and dad.'

Jamie grinned at last. She reminded him of Mum. Mum always bothered whether people had had enough to eat and drink.

Quickly he turned his head away in case the policewoman should see the tears glistening in his eyes . . .

★ ★ ★

'He's on his way.' The police sergeant at Victoria poked his head into the interview room where Leon, Rosa and William sat in awkward silence. 'And a word of advice, for what it's worth. Save the recriminations for later. Just be thankful you've got him back unscathed. You can hold the inquest when you're all less fraught.'

'Yes, of course. And thanks,' Leon said gratefully.

William stood up. 'Now we know he's OK, I'll make myself scarce.' He paused awkwardly. 'You'll — er — all go back in Dad's car anyway, won't you?'

Rosa and Leon looked at each other, then nodded. 'Yes, good idea.' Leon said. 'We're going to have to present a united front.'

'William, thank you.' Rosa squeezed his hand. 'I couldn't have coped without you.'

'You've got Dad now. Just get Jamie

back home safe and sound.'

With a tired smile, William left the brightly-lit room, and Rosa and Leon found themselves alone together for the first time since their separation.

'That sergeant was right,' Rosa said warningly. 'We'll sort things out later. Don't blow your top the minute Jamie walks through the door.'

'Me? Since when have I been the heavy father?'

'Since when have you been any sort of father — except an absent one?' The hurtful words had left her lips before she had time to think.

'I'm well aware of my shortcomings, but I've only ever tried to give you all everything you wanted. If that meant spending time away, then — '

'Maybe if you'd spent more time attending Jamie's school things, or taking an interest in his football, instead of trying to recapture your youth and build a business empire at the same time, we wouldn't be here tonight.'

'Leave it, Rosa. This is neither the

time nor the place to be discussing our problems. We both know what has happened and why. Now the most important thing is to make sure that none of the children suffers further because of it.'

'At last.' Rosa's smile was sad. 'Something we agree on.'

'We used to agree on everything.' Leon sighed softly. 'When did we start drifting apart?'

'Goodness knows.' She stared at her hands. 'Probably long before you became embroiled with Brennan and Foulkes and the Four Seasons. And Felicity Phelps . . . '

Felicity . . . Leon thought about Felicity. She seemed so much part of his present and his future — far more vividly real than Rosa, his wife. He wanted to wish that he had never met her, but he couldn't.

'Mr and Mrs Brodie.' The door had opened and Jamie's policewoman popped her curly head into the room. 'Your wanderer has returned.'

Trying to be brave, Jamie stared at his parents as they rose to their feet. They looked tired and frightened, not angry. And they were together. With a hoarse cry, the child inside him defeated the teenager's bravado and he stumbled into their outstretched arms.

'Just a few formalities,' the policewoman said quietly, 'and then you can all go home to bed.'

'Home?' Jamie raised his white face to his parents. 'Are we all going home together?'

Rosa and Leon exchanged glances across his head.

'Dad's driving us all back to Highcliffe, yes,' Rosa said quietly.

It probably wasn't exactly the reassurance that he wanted, but it was the truth. And it would have to do for now.

★   ★   ★

'He's asleep.' Rosa turned back to the front of the car as Leon drove swiftly along the motorway. 'I don't think I'll

183

ever sleep again.'

'Nor me.' Leon concentrated fiercely on the road ahead. 'And you were right, Rosa. If I'm going to be an absent father officially, then I'm going to have to make more time for each of the kids. I've relied on William's good nature with the Nook, trusted that Kizzy's self-reliance would see her through, and Jamie — ' He sighed. 'I suppose I left Jamie to you.'

'We can talk about this later.' Rosa swallowed. 'I'm seeing Paul Beatty about the financial and legal business. I'm determined to hang on to my share of the Nook, you know that. Once I'm assured that we'll still have a roof over our heads, then we'll make arrangements for the children. And we'll never risk another episode like this one . . . '

'Definitely not,' Leon said fervently. 'Look, I know we're shattered and distraught and not thinking particularly clearly, but if I found someone to buy out my half of the Nook, would that make things easier for you?'

'Have you got someone in mind?' she asked.

'Yes. Someone who has been right under my nose. Someone I know would run it as well, if not better, than me.'

'Are we home yet?' Jamie stirred on the back seat and raised his head.

Rosa gave Leon a warning glance, and smiled at Jamie.

'Yes, love. Only a few more minutes.'

'Good.' Jamie said. 'Nearly home — then we'll all be together again . . . '

A Rock To Lean On

The morning was warm and golden. Rosa sat on the weather-worn bench on the cliff top and watched as the grey of the sea melted mistily into the flax flower blue of the sky. Behind her, Highcliffe was slowly coming to life. She let the gentle breeze pull at her hair, welcoming its freshness.

Kizzy was still sleeping, no doubt dreaming of Andrew and weddings and happy-ever-afters. A note on the kitchen pin board had announced his unexpected arrival.

Jamie was asleep, too. Rosa had peeped into his room, and noticed the trails of tears streaking his cheeks. Had they been shed in London? Or in the early hours when he'd realised that Leon wouldn't be sleeping at the house?

Together they had gently explained to

him, although Rosa would have happily agreed to Leon's staying if it meant Jamie's face losing that haunted look.

Jamie, too exhausted to fight any more, had nodded dumbly and collapsed into bed and Leon had left. Rosa had felt she had never disliked him more than at that moment when he closed the door behind him.

She gave another sigh. At least there were William and Lisa — not to mention Lewis and Otis. She had left them in the garden, Lewis gurgling contentedly in his buggy while William and Lisa chased the ever-exuberant Otis around the garden, their laughter echoing into the house.

Rosa thanked God for that laughter. It was a long time since Honeysuckle House had had anything to laugh about.

★　★　★

Leon was just waking, screwing up his eyes against the sun that was poking intrusive fingers through the blinds. Felicity's cream leather sofa, which had seemed the last word in luxury when he'd collapsed on to it last night, now seemed cramped and uncomfortable.

'Good morning, sleepyhead.' Felicity drifted into the room in a swathe of peach silk, carrying a tray of freshly-squeezed orange juice and wholemeal rolls warm from the oven. Leon smiled at her sleepily, loving her, but treacherously wishing for one of Rosa's Sunday morning fry-ups.

'I didn't want to wake you last night.' He struggled into a sitting position, feeling unkempt and unshaven.

'I was just delighted to find you here this morning. It meant that Jamie had been brought home safely.' She perched on the edge of the sofa, watching him eat. 'And that you'd chosen to come here rather than stay at Honeysuckle House or go to Steven's . . . '

'Jamie wanted me to stay at the house,' he admitted, 'but it would have been wrong to begin a pretence that

I've no intention of continuing. He's safe. That's the main thing.'

'I'm so glad.' Felicity smiled tenderly. 'You were never out of my thoughts last night. I was quite busy, too, though. I've arranged meetings for tomorrow. If you can definitely find a buyer for your half of the Nook, it looks as if we can go ahead with the purchase of the Old Granary.'

'That's great.' Leon took her hand, 'because I've already found one . . .'

*   *   *

Rosa's thoughts had drifted, in time with the fat white clouds now skimming the skyline, away from her immediate family. She, too, was thinking of the Nook. If Leon had a buyer for his share of the Nook, it would make tomorrow's meeting with Paul Beatty easier.

She would still have to find some means of supporting herself, but if someone else was willing to take over the day-to-day running of the Nook, leaving William as chef, then that would bring some financial security. But who would want to buy into half a business? Carl and Marcia?

'I take it that things are better with your world this morning?'

The quiet voice made her jump. Steven stood behind the bench, his hair lifted by the breeze, his eyes gentle.

'Yes. Much.' She smiled.

'Thanks for your phone call last night. I'm glad it was a happy ending.'

'More a tricky beginning.' Rosa squinted against the sun. 'I shall have to keep an eye on Jamie — but at least Leon has agreed to spend more time with him. We've agreed — ' she laughed at the word ' — to become model parents for Jamie's sake. Separated, but united in our love for the children.'

'Good.' Steven sat down beside her. 'And the rest of the brood?'

'All right, I think. William and Lisa are playing happy families, and Andrew turned up last night so no doubt we'll be hearing about nothing but the wedding from that quarter. No, Jamie's the one being most hurt by all this . . . '

'Apart from you.'

'Apart from me.' She returned his smile, relaxing, listening to the gentle waves on the shingle.

'You look lovely.' His voice seemed to rise and fall with the waves.

'I look a scruff!' she retorted.

'Don't argue.' Steven laughed with her. 'You're beautiful.'

'Maybe I'll become a supermodel, then.' She grinned, feeling absurdly young and lighthearted after the traumas of the last few days.

She turned to him, suddenly serious. 'Leon mentioned that he might have found a buyer for his half of the Nook. Has he said anything to you?'

'Yes.' Steven looked away, his eyes following a boat on the horizon. 'I didn't say anything earlier because you were so worried about Jamie, but yes, he has. It's me. He's offered me the chance to become your partner . . . '

She gaped at him. 'You! What do you

know about restaurants — apart from eating your way through the menu and ordering the best wines?'

'Absolutely nothing.' He grinned. 'And that's the way I intend to keep it. I shall be a sleeping partner, buying out Leon's share and putting William in full control — which, goodness knows, he deserves. I've no intention of interfering with the way Cookery Nook operates. I just thought it would help you out of one of your dilemmas.'

Rosa stood up, the wind from the sea wrapping her long cotton skirt about her legs. 'You didn't have some ulterior motive?'

'Such as?' Steven's voice was low.

'Well — Leon is your friend. Buying out his share in the Nook will enable him and Felicity Phelps to go ahead with the Four Seasons, won't it? Also — ' she added quickly, as he was about to speak, ' — it means that you and I can be seen together without raising eyebrows, doesn't it?'

For a minute he gazed out over the

tumbling waves, then he turned to face her.

'Leon will finance the Four Seasons somehow — you know that as well as I do. And if he'd raised the money through loans, what would that do for your security? They'd use the Nook as collateral, and you could lose everything. If he sold it to a stranger who might not want a mere half interest in it, who's to say they'd keep William on? If I buy Leon's share, it'll be for one reason only — to keep you and the children safe . . . '

Rosa believed him, and she was grateful to him. It was just . . . 'What about the other reason?'

'Being seen together without tongues wagging?' His eyes crinkled at the corners. 'What do you think?'

She was unable to stop her own smile matching his. 'You're impossible!'

'So I've been told.' He moved towards her and rested his hands on her shoulders. 'So, Mrs Brodie, if I become your business partner — and I stress 'business' — do I take it you'll raise no objections?'

'Better the devil you know, I suppose,' she agreed. 'It's certainly better for William. And I can carry on with my plans to keep the family afloat.'

She turned her head, avoiding his eyes. Knowing how he felt about her, she was still too vulnerable to allow him to weaken her newly-found resolve. Let Leon and Felicity throw themselves into the love affair of the century, she thought wearily. I'm the one who's going to keep home and family together — and I don't want complications like Steven Casey making my knees go weak . . .

'Ah, yes, your plans.' Sensing her reserve, Steven dropped his hands. 'Have you decided what you're going to do?'

'Actually, yes.' Rosa pushed her wayward hair behind her ears. 'I'll have to go through the pros and cons with Paul Beatty, of course, but the answer has been staring me in the face all the time.'

'Which is?'

'You'll have to wait and see,' she teased him. 'Maybe we'll have a business meeting to discuss it. I believe Leon's always found business meetings very useful!'

'You must feel a whole lot better when you can make a joke about it.'

'Who's joking?' she retorted over her shoulder. 'I mean it. We'll have a business meeting tomorrow evening, after I've been to the bank. Come up to the house about half-past seven, and I'll cook a meal.'

'What about Jamie?'

'I'll explain things to Jamie. Once he accepts that Leon has left because he wants to — ' She shrugged. 'Well, I'm sure he'll understand.'

'And you'd give it all up tomorrow if Leon would come back, wouldn't you?'

Rosa paused and turned to face him. 'I — I honestly don't think so. Anyway, why speculate on the impossible?

Leon's made it quite clear that Felicity offers him a future he could never find with us.'

'He's a fool.' Steven slid his arm companionably round her shoulders. 'Hey, isn't that love's young dream thundering through the undergrowth?'

Rosa grinned. Kizzy, her hair flying, was running full pelt towards them.

'Hi, Mum — Steven.' Kizzy panted to a halt. 'Oh, don't look so panicky. Jamie's asleep, the house hasn't burned down, William and Lisa are feeding Lewis, and I'm just off to visit Andrew's parents. They've invited me for lunch, and then we're going to discuss the wedding . . . '

'And?' Rosa prompted, knowing her daughter.

'And what?' Kizzy scuffed at the path, sending up a dusty cloud.

'And where's the inner glow that prospective brides are supposed to have? Or at least some sort of twinkle in your eye because Andrew's back in Highcliffe? What's wrong, love?'

'Nothing. I don't think it's sunk in yet, that's all.' Kizzy twisted her fingers in a stray curl. 'I expect I'll feel better when I've spoken to his parents. I do love him, Mum — it's just — ' She broke off.

'If you have any doubts at all, darling, don't be pressurised into anything you don't want to do. Look, come back home and we'll talk.'

'Later. Let me go and see them all first. I want to see what Mr Pearson has done with the chalet, and what plans Andrew has for turning the nursery into a garden centre. And to see where I'm supposed to fit into all this.'

Rosa watched her go. 'That is not a happy girl,' she said to Steven. 'She looks so defeated, somehow.'

'You've all been through a lot.' Steven followed Rosa's eyes. 'Perhaps Kizzy views marriage and happy-ever-afters with a bit more cynicism now, and who can blame her? Maybe they'll postpone the wedding.'

'I hope they do, honestly. But I don't

want her to finish with Andrew altogether just because of what's happened to us. Leon had no idea what he was doing to this family when he took up with Felicity.'

★   ★   ★

'It's one thing after another with your lot at the moment, isn't it?' Norma Beatty pushed her gardening hat further back on her head, and nodded towards Jamie, pottering about in the borders. 'He looks happier though.'

Rosa lifted her face to the dappled sunshine. 'I told him he could have some friends round, but he chose to come here with me. I think he'll be a bit shaken up for a while — and this is his second home.'

'Poor little mite.' Norma smiled fondly at Jamie's thin frame, hair fashionably spiked, as he dextrously replanted the unwieldy mallow bushes. 'He was probably more frightened about being in London than any of you.

198

He'll have learned his lesson. And if he doesn't make it as a footballer, he'll always be able to make a living as a gardener.'

'He's certainly got green fingers, even if it is unfashionable. All his friends seem to want to work with computers. Still . . . ' She moved along the bench to give Norma room. 'I just want them all to be happy.'

'And they will be.' Norma nodded. 'You and Leon are good parents. You've given them the right values. Even if you're not together, they'll still have that rock to lean on.'

Rosa glanced across at Jamie, completely immersed in his gardening. He seemed more settled. He'd even agreed quite eagerly to Steven coming to dinner, when Rosa had explained that it would mean the Nook would continue as before if Steven became a partner. Gently, she'd elaborated on Leon's plans for the Old Granary, allowing Jamie to work out that his dad really had left home for good, but that he would still be part of their lives.

'Just think,' she'd said, with far more enthusiasm than she felt, 'when Dad opens the Four Seasons you'll have two places to go and be fed!'

'Will they do burgers?' Jamie had asked. 'Dad and William never did burgers at the Nook.'

'You'll have to ask him. I expect they'll have a fast food outlet somewhere in the complex.'

'Brill!' Jamie's eyes were shining. 'Maybe I could even work there at weekends or something. Then I could save enough money for the school football tour next summer. That'd be really mega . . . '

Yes! Rosa nodded to herself in the sleepy garden. Jamie was recovering with all the resilience of youth.

'Oh, Rosa, we were clearing out the conservatory and I wondered if Kizzy would like those cane chairs?' Norma waved a hand towards them. 'They'd look really nice with a few new cushions.'

'I'm sure she'd love them,' Rosa agreed. 'She's probably planning her new home at this very minute . . . '

★   ★   ★

At that very minute, Kizzy was glaring at Andrew in something like fury.

'No! No way! I can't agree to it!'

'But why not?' Andrew shook his head. 'Mum and Dad have been so helpful, and with all the fuss in your family I'm sure they only thought they were acting for the best . . . '

'They're taking over!' Kizzy wailed. 'Can't you see? Because you've been away in Edinburgh for so long, they've got used to making your decisions for you. But they're not going to make mine!'

'They're not trying to!'

'Yes, they are. It's all cut and dried! For goodness' sake — I'm not even out of school yet. I don't want to be tied to a kitchen sink — let alone your mother's kitchen sink — yet, if ever!

You and your dad to run the garden centre while I help your mother about the house — become a diligent little housewife in rubber gloves and a frilly apron? No, thank you!'

'They didn't mean it like that! They only said — '

'That once we're married I should have 'some time to get used to things' and you and your dad should do the 'men's work' . . . '

'What's wrong with that?'

'Everything!' Kizzy turned tear-filled eyes to him. 'We were going to run the garden centre, Andrew. You and me. I was going to do the accounts, the publicity, while you fronted the operation. As partners. That was the whole idea. That was why you went to college. Wasn't it?'

'But Dad doesn't want to relinquish the reins yet — and it is his business. I can't just step in and say, thanks for getting it off the ground but your way is hopelessly old fashioned, so just leave it to me and Kizzy now, can I?'

'I know that. I don't want you to hurt them — but this is my life we're talking about.'

'Our life,' Andrew said softly, pulling her against him. 'You seem to have forgotten the 'our', Kizzy. You've changed.'

'So have you!' She pulled away from him. 'You've changed so much that you've forgotten our dreams.'

'The dreams were the only thing that made Edinburgh bearable.' He sighed. 'Dreaming of coming back to High-cliffe and putting all that theory into practice. Having the best garden centre in the area — with you as my wife. And now, because your father has decided to leave home, you're behaving like a stranger. What do you want, Kizzy?'

'I don't know!' The cry was despairing. 'But I know what I don't want. I don't want to be a clone of your mother, always fussing about dusting the skirting boards. And I don't want to be a clone of mine, either, throwing away the best part of my life on a mistake!'

'So I'm a mistake, am I?' Andrew's voice was dangerously cold.

'I don't know. I don't know anything any more.'

Andrew looked at the chalet, so lovingly refurbished by his father, at the rooms that, in a few months, he and Kizzy were supposed to be living in as husband and wife. At the stuff of his dreams.

'So what do you think we should do?' His heart was in his mouth.

'If I had an engagement ring,' Kizzy said, 'I'd give it back to you. As it is, I think we'd better forget it, Andrew. I can't marry you.'

★   ★   ★

'And when did all this happen?' Leon looked at Kizzy across the table. 'Yesterday.' Kizzy steadied her trembling lip and concentrated on her coffee. 'He only came back two days

204

ago — and now I've ruined it . . . '

'No, you haven't.' Leon reached out and clasped her hand. 'True, you might have been more diplomatic — but you've never been noted for your tact, darling, have you? Both you and Andrew have been living on dreams for so long.'

'I must have inherited that from you, then.' Kizzy looked at him. 'That's what you do, isn't it?'

Leon sighed. 'I deserved that! What have I done to you?'

'Made me open my eyes.' Kizzy sniffed. 'This hasn't been that sudden, Dad. As soon as I knew about you and Mum, I started feeling different. Scared. I — I was in love with the idea of being in love . . . I didn't look any further than the wedding and swanning about in a beautiful white dress.'

'Do you love Andrew?'

'I always have! It's not that. I just want to be me first, before I become the next Mrs Pearson. I'm not ready for all the things Andrew's mum finds so important. I want to be me.'

Leon sat back and looked at this daughter he loved to distraction. And she had chosen to tell him, not Rosa. He felt a warm glow about that, after fearing he'd lost her confidence for ever.

'Has Andrew been in touch since you stormed out?'

'No. I couldn't go to school. So I waited till Mum went out, then I rang you. Is it always going to be like this? Meeting in cafés? I mean, where are you living?'

'Officially, still at Steven's,' Leon said quickly, 'but I spend more time at Felicity's. Would you come and see me there?'

'I don't know. I suppose so. I mean — I don't really want to meet her, but that's not being very grown-up, is it? Oh, Dad . . . What should I do?'

'I'm probably the worst person in the world to give advice, but I think you should go and see Andrew. Tell him you're sorry for hurting him, but that you need time to think things over. Leave things until after your exams. Andrew's a great bloke, Kizzy. He'll understand. Just concentrate on your exams, and then once the pressure's off you may see things differently . . . '

'He'll probably never want to see me again!'

'Maybe not, at first. But he'll come round. Just be brave, and stay true to your heart.'

'Like you?' She stared at him.

'Kizzy, I loved your mother desperately. We were just as young and idealistic as you and Andrew, and we had so many years of being happy. That's more than a lot of people can say.'

Kizzy took a deep breath. 'But would you still have left Mum even if you hadn't fallen out over the Four Seasons? Even if you hadn't met — ' she swallowed ' — Felicity?'

That was a question Leon had asked himself many times during those long, lonely hours of darkness when sleep evaded him.

'Yes. Yes, I would.'

'Thanks, Dad.' She stood up quickly. 'I'll get the bus back to Highcliffe and go and see Andrew, make him understand how I feel. And — and let me know when you move in to Felicity's flat. I'll need the number . . . '

Five minutes later, Felicity dropped into the seat Kizzy had so recently vacated. 'Penny for them?' she said.

'I'll never cease to be amazed by my kids.' Leon kissed her. 'I think Kizzy and I have just become friends again.'

'Good. And did you give her the right advice?'

'Goodness knows.' Leon sighed. 'But I told her the truth. I told her to follow her heart.'

'And does she know about us? About you moving in? Or was it not the right time to tell her?'

'No, I told her. She accepted it quite calmly. She's growing up very quickly. I'd like you two to be friends.'

'So would I.' Felicity squeezed his

hand. 'Very much. But we'll let her make all the moves. Now, do you want to hear about the meeting?'

Leon sat for a moment, watching her face. This was the last vestige of the past. On her words his future depended, a future that no longer included the Nook, or Honeysuckle House, or Rosa. The future would be Felicity and the Four Seasons . . .

'With Steven Casey's offer confirmed, Brennan and Foulkes are more than happy to back you financially. In fact,' she tapped her briefcase, 'their projected cash input is higher than our most optimistic figure. On your behalf, Leon, Brennan and Foulkes have just purchased the Old Granary.'

Holding On To The Past

Rosa lit the candles, then blew them out. Candles were synonymous with romance, and she didn't want to give Steven the wrong idea about this dinner. She switched on the table lamps instead.

For the twentieth time, she looked at her reflection in the mirror. She hadn't taken this much care with her appearance for a long time. Her hair gleamed, her silk dress was flattering, and she'd even bothered with mascara and lipstick. Just to raise her own spirits, she told herself. Absolutely nothing to do with Steven. After all, he'd seen her around for years in jeans and Leon's shirts, her face bare . . . She didn't need to pretend for him.

She checked the cooker. Everything was ready. Of course, the menu wouldn't be up to that of the Nook. It was one of the drawbacks of being married to a chef — her own culinary skills had taken a back seat.

Tonight had given her an opportunity to shine — in more ways than one.

When the bell rang she flew to answer it, more like Kizzy than a middle-aged mother. Her stomach was full of aerobic butterflies.

'Rosa — you look sensational!' Steven handed her a bottle of wine and a bunch of stately, deep-blue irises. 'Are you expecting someone?'

'I always dress for dinner!' She laughed, feeling absurdly happy for the first time in ages. 'And you don't look so bad yourself.'

'It probably wouldn't pass muster in the Savoy.' He glanced down at his neatly-pressed trousers, smart shirt and tie. 'But for an out-and-out scruff it's the best I can do. Something smells wonderful! All your own work?'

'Every scrap.' She showed him into the dining-room. 'I hope you're hungry. I've forgotten what it's like to cook for two — I've done far too much.'

'I'm starving.' He lowered himself into the rocking-chair and looked at the two place-settings. 'And it's just us, is it? Am I being shunned by your children?'

'Not at all. William's on duty at the Nook, and Lisa has gone in with him to waitress. We're baby-sitting both Lewis and the dog. Kizzy has gone to her mate Fiona's to do some revision, and Jamie is with three of his friends being spoiled rotten with burgers and beans at the Beattys.'

She indicated the flowers. 'Just let me find a vase, then we can eat.'

'Do you want a hand?'

'No, just sit there and relax — I'll be back in a minute.'

'I could get used to this,' he said softly as Rosa darted through to the kitchen. 'Leon Brodie, you are the most foolish man in the world!'

★   ★   ★

'More potatoes?' Rosa looked across the table. 'Or cauliflower cheese?'

'No, thank you.' Steven laid down his knife and fork. 'I couldn't eat another mouthful . . . '

'Not even bread and butter pudding?'

'Temptress!' He groaned. 'How did you know I can never say no to that?'

'A wild guess.' She grinned, raising her glass. 'Anyway, here's to the continuation of Cookery Nook.'

Steven chinked his glass against hers, rainbows dancing from the crystal.

'To a long and happy partnership. Mind you, I think I'll be putting you in place of William as chef,' he joked.

'Oh, I think the eaters at the Nook expect more than steak and kidney and bread and butter pudding! My basic skills in the kitchen may come in handy, though.' She regarded him through the golden glow of her wine glass. 'I'm going to turn Honeysuckle House into a B and B . . . '

'But it's your home! How can you bear to have it filled with strangers?'

'Exactly. It's my home. It's where I want to stay and it's what I do best. Run a home, feed people, make them comfortable. I told you it was staring me in the face. I discussed it with Paul Beatty today, and my solicitor's drawing up all the paperwork. There are rules and regulations, of course, but I want to be up and running in time for the summer season.

'And how can I bear to fill my home with strangers?' She stared into his eyes. 'Rather that than losing it altogether. I've lost Leon — I'm not going to lose my home!'

He smiled tenderly at her. 'You're wonderful, Rosa. What can I say?'

'Say that this is not the most stupid notion you've ever heard, that it's not just a crazy dream that will lead to bankruptcy . . . '

'Rosa Brodie, you are the most brilliant, beautiful, resourceful woman in the whole world — and you deserve a kiss!'

Laughing, he pulled her towards him

as she protested mildly.

'I said this should never happen again. It isn't why I invited you.'

'I know,' he said softly. 'I know.'

Neither of them heard the key in the latch. Neither heard the footsteps in the hall. Neither of them heard the dining-room door open softly.

'What the devil's going on?' Leon's shout made them spring apart. 'I can't believe this!'

'What can't you believe?' Rosa moved away from Steven and met her husband's eyes. 'That because you compared me with Felicity and found me wanting, no other man could possibly find me attractive? Well, it came as a bit of a shock to me, too. You'd done a pretty good job of undermining my confidence. But thanks to Steven — '

'Steven is my friend!' Leon growled. 'And you are my wife!'

'I'm sorry if you don't like the situation, Leon, but you left me, and this house and the children, remember?

Still — ' She swallowed. 'I will admit I made a mistake. My mistake,' she continued icily, 'was to allow you to keep your key. Without that you would have phoned first and I could have told you that tonight wasn't convenient.'

'But you were kissing!' Leon realised he was jealous.

'Of course we were kissing!' Rosa was close to tears. 'We were celebrating our business partnership which means that Cookery Nook will still be a viable proposition when you and Felicity are holding court in the Four Seasons! A partnership that means I can run my own business and keep this roof over our heads. That's why we were kissing, Leon. For the first time in ages I felt happy and secure and could see some sort of future.'

'We were also kissing,' Steven put in, 'because Rosa is a very lovely lady who should be kissed often. She needs hugs, love and laughter — all somewhat neglected of late.'

'The breakdown of our marriage is

none of your concern!' Leon snapped.

'Since when?' Steven sat down in the rocking-chair. 'I've been a friend to you both for as long as I can remember. I've heard both sides of this story. I've told you from the start that you're a fool for doing what you've done. And Rosa . . .' He reached up and caught her trembling hand. 'Rosa knows how I feel about her — but,' he went on quickly, 'she has always discouraged me from taking my feelings further. She's loyal to you, Leon, even after the way you've behaved.'

'Are you telling me that you're in love with her?'

An indignant yell spiralled down the staircase, followed by a volley of gruff barking. If only Otis had stirred earlier when Leon had silently turned his key in the lock!

'It's the baby,' Rosa said unnecessarily. 'I'll go . . .'

'No.' Steven rose. 'I will. Leon came to talk to you, so I'll get out of the way.' He paused in the doorway and looked at Leon. 'And since you ask . . . yes, I am in love with Rosa.'

Blushing, Rosa faced her husband across the table. 'Why did you come?'

'To tell you that I've bought the Old Granary. I didn't want you to hear it on the grapevine. I came to discuss it with you and the kids. I came to see if Jamie was OK, and if Kizzy had sorted things with Andrew. I came because I thought that was what we had agreed . . . '

'Oh, Leon!' Rosa sighed. 'I think we'll have to make it a rule to ring each other in future, don't you? After all, we're leading separate lives.'

'What if it had been Jamie who walked in on you?'

Rosa sat down. 'Jamie knew Steven was coming to supper. I told Kizzy and William, too. The children were perfectly happy with the arrangement — just as they're equally happy with my plans for Honeysuckle House.'

'What plans?' He frowned.

'I was going to ring you tomorrow and tell you. I'm turning the house into a B and B . . . '

'Over my dead body!' He leapt to his feet. 'I will not have hordes of holidaymakers traipsing all over my house, leaving sand in the carpets and seaweed in the sinks . . . What are you laughing at?'

'You! You're priceless! You don't live here any more, remember? You live in Felicity Phelps' luxury apartment at Dawley marina. And there's absolutely nothing you can do to stop me making Honeysuckle House the best bed and breakfast establishment in Highcliffe! I thought you might be pleased. If I can be big enough to congratulate you on the Four Seasons, I would have thought you could at least return the compliment.'

He moved closer and placed both hands on her shoulders, and gazed at her face, as if memorising its every feature. Rosa gazed back, transfixed. They had been through so much together, but in future their lives would barely touch.

She could hear the sea restlessly crashing outside in the darkness, hear the distant whimpers of Lewis, and Steven's deep, soothing voice, hear the beating of her own heart.

She pulled away from his grip. 'What are you trying to do, Leon?'

'Hold on to the past, I suppose.' He shrugged. 'Sometimes I wish . . . '

'It's too late for regrets now. The changes you have made are irrevocable. You'll never change, Leon. You'll always want to chase dreams.'

He nodded slowly, then: 'Are you in love with Steven?'

'No!' then she paused. 'Well . . . I've always loved him as a friend. It's too soon to tell if what I feel now is love or gratitude. I'm the cautious one, remember? I don't plunge into anything without thinking it through.' She looked at him. 'Why? Does it matter to you?'

'It might. One of the reasons I came here tonight — in fact, the main reason — was to suggest that we should

consider making our separation permanent. And official.'

The distant sound of the sea had
become a deafening roar in her ears.

'You mean divorce,' Rosa said dully.

★   ★   ★

Kizzy pushed her way into the Nook
and dropped ungracefully into a chair
near the kitchen. It was always the last
table to be taken, and tonight, early on
Thursday evening, the restaurant was
barely half full.

Nothing was going right. The A-levels
which had seemed so distant were now
only weeks away. Andrew had curtly
refused to see her or even speak to her
on the phone. The plans to turn
Honeysuckle House into a B and B.
were galloping into reality, and the
house was swarming with builders and
surveyors and men with clipboards.
And her parents, each of them seeking
her out and telling her as gently as
possible, were considering divorce.

Part of Kizzy had always thought that when her dad tired of his new life, he'd come back home. It had never once occurred to her that Mum might not want him back, or that Leon really wanted to make the parting permanent.

'Hi, Kizzy. Are you here to eat or did you want to see William?' One of the waitresses paused beside the table. 'Shall I give him a shout?'

'Please — if he's not too busy . . . '

'William's always busy.' The girl grinned. 'Still, at least he's in charge now — not like when your dad — er . . . '

'It's OK.' Kizzy smiled. 'I know what you mean.'

It was a week since Steven had bought Leon out of the Nook. Apart from paper shuffling, there were no obvious signs of change. Carl and Marcia still happily worked the lunch-time openings, William planned menus and followed Leon's recipes and, with a little encouragement from Lisa, was trying out some dishes of his own.

Kizzy glanced at the menu. Some of the meals were really quite innovative. Lisa's influence?'

'I can recommend the monkfish.' William dropped down opposite her, chef's whites stained, hair awry. 'If you're ordering . . . '

'I'm not. I'm looking for sanctuary. The house is like bedlam. All my friends are swotting like crazy, and I can't go to Andrew's any more . . .

'Anyway, Dad always did monkfish.' She held up the menu. 'But he didn't do fillet of red bream with pimento and rosemary risotto, or artichokes with warm goat's cheese, or any of these sauces — black olive and caper, lemongrass, spinach and saffron . . . '

'Lisa's suggestions.' He grinned proudly. 'She feels we should do fewer red meat and conventional dishes. More and more people are sticking to white meat and fish these days.' He paused, noticing Kizzy's bleak eyes. 'Still, you didn't come here to talk about Lisa. What's bothering you? Is it

Mum and Dad?'

'Not really.' She shook her head. 'I was shocked when they told me about the divorce — I mean, it's all happened so quickly. But it's up to them. I don't have any childish dreams of last-minute reunions or anything — I just wish they weren't so selfish!'

'Selfish?' William had been gazing round the Nook, noting with satisfaction that the tables were filling nicely, but that brought his attention back to his sister. 'Mum has never been selfish in her life! And Dad . . . well, Dad's just Dad. He's always been the same. He comes up with these crazy notions, and it never occurs to him that they might not be what everyone else wants to do.'

'Maybe I don't mean selfish,' Kizzy said. 'Life is just so upside down! By the time the Four Seasons is up and running we'll be living in a B and B. — and it'll all be happening when I should have been getting married.'

Fat teardrops slid silently down her cheeks. William handed her a napkin.

'Don't cry, Kizz. Look, Lisa will be in soon. Suppose she takes the night off and you can have an evening out together? Go into Dawley or something. How about ten-pin bowling? You used to enjoy that.'

'When I went with Andrew.' She sniffed. 'Oh, William, I wish he'd speak to me at least . . . '

'Do you want me to talk to him? We've always been good mates — and he's bound to be as unhappy as you are. Maybe if I explain to him that you just want to postpone the wedding for a while . . . '

She groaned. 'How can I think about weddings when Mum and Dad are splitting up? I just . . . I just want Andrew back!'

This time her tears crumpled her face. William stroked her hair.

'Stop it, Kizz. Please. People will think I've poisoned you with the garlic bread or something! I promise, no wedding talk. But let me ring him.'

'All right,' Kizzy wiped her eyes. 'But

later, when I'm not here. And yes, I'd enjoy an evening out with Lisa.'

'For you — anything.' He grinned. 'I hate the idea of the divorce, too. But at least they talk to each other more now.'

'I know. Oh, I understand that love doesn't last for ever, but I still wanted to believe that it did. Even Jamie seems to have accepted it more than me — all he's going on about is working in the burger bar when Dad opens the Four Seasons.' She gave a wan smile. 'Have you met Felicity Phelps yet?'

'I'm not sure that I want to,' he admitted, 'but maybe we'll have to. After all, if the divorce goes through, he might want to marry her.'

'He couldn't! Could he?'

'Who knows with Dad?' His eyes suddenly lit up as the door opened and he rose to hug Lisa. 'Do you fancy a girls' night out with Kizzy?'

'Oh, lovely!' She beamed at them. 'It's ages since I had an evening off. Where are we going? Into Dawley?'

'If you like.' Kizzy got to her feet.

'William, you won't forget to ring Andrew, will you?'

'Cross my heart.' He winked at her.

Lisa stood on tiptoe to kiss William goodbye. 'Actually, you're not the only one who can spring surprises. I've got one for you, too.'

William groaned. 'I've experienced your surprises before. Lewis — Otis — not to mention that dragon of a landlady! How bad is this one?'

'That depends on your definition of bad.' Her smile was impish now. 'We both have tomorrow off, don't we?'

'Yes ... What have you got in mind?'

'How would you like to spend it meeting my parents?' she asked.

* * *

Leon stretched out on the sofa, wriggling the downy cushions more comfortably behind his head, and concentrated on the phone.

'Sounds like a great idea. You're sure

that's what he really wants to do?'

'So he says,' Rosa's light voice told him. 'Is it all right to talk, Leon? Is Felicity there?'

'No, she isn't, and even if she were, you know you can ring at any time. Especially about the children. You're all right?'

'Up to my ears in building regulations and quotes for partitions and conversions and goodness knows what else.' He could tell she was smiling. 'But at least all this upheaval means I can give the housework a miss. Actually, I'm quite enjoying myself.'

'You sound great.' Leon's voice was surprised. 'Maybe you should have done something like this years ago.'

'No, I don't think so. It doesn't come naturally to me. I'm heaps better at being a — ' She stopped. 'I was going to say wife and mother, but perhaps homemaker is a better description.'

'I think you were right the first time,' Leon said softly. 'You were the best wife any man could wish for . . . '

'Stop it! You didn't think so at the time, did you?'

'I always thought so.'

There was silence for a moment.

'So you'll tell Jamie we'll do that?' Leon was the first to speak. 'He can take half a dozen of his friends to Laserquest for his birthday and then on to the Pizza Palace. And you're sure he wants us there? I didn't want my parents hanging around on my fifteenth birthday.'

'I'm sure you didn't, but he's still very vulnerable. He wants us to be there — together.'

'Not Felicity — or Steven?'

'Not even Kizzy and William. And don't lump Steven into the same category as Felicity, please.'

'No. Sorry. Well, that's fine. Tell him I'll buy him the biggest pizza in the place and beat him at the Laserquest.'

'I'll tell him. I'll have to go. I'm child and dog-sitting and they both want feeding. Kizzy has gone out and William and Lisa are both working

— and it'd take more than me to prise Jamie away from his new computer game.'

'OK. I'll ring you soon. Take care.'

Leon put the receiver down and glanced at his watch. Felicity should be in soon. She'd been at a meeting in Birmingham, and it was now nearly eight o'clock. This was something he was getting used to, being alone in the flat. Coming home to nothing but this elegant apartment, with its pale woods and carpets and soft, pastel drapes.

This flat was Felicity, sophisticated and elegant, just as Honeysuckle House was all Rosa, flowers and warmth, cluttered with the possessions of a lifetime.

How long would it take him not to listen for the children as he unlocked the door? How long would it be before he didn't look for Rosa, emerging flushed and smiling from the kitchen? But looking back through rose-tinted spectacles wouldn't do. That picture was from long ago. It was far too late to rekindle the flames.

He heard Felicity's key in the door, then she was there, dropping her briefcase on the floor and crossing the room to nestle in his arms. 'Hi! Oh, I'm shattered. The traffic was a nightmare.' She pushed her face into his shoulder, luxuriating in his warmth. She loved coming home to him.

'Sit down. I'll get you a glass of wine . . . '

'You're wonderful.' She eased her feet from the high-heeled shoes. 'Just let me unwind a bit, and then I'll have a shower and we'll go out to eat.'

Leon brought her glass across. 'I'll cook if you like.'

'No. That's not fair. We'll go down to that new place on the waterfront.'

'But I'm not working — I haven't worked all week,' Leon protested.

'Make the most of it!' Felicity laughed, sipping her drink. 'Things should start moving on the Old Granary by next Wednesday. You won't have a spare moment after that!'

'Next Wednesday? As soon as that?' Then he paused. 'Oh, no . . . '

'What's wrong?'

'Wednesday. I've got something else on.'

'Something more important than a planning meeting with the architects?'

'I'm afraid so.' Leon slid his hands under the silky fall of her hair. 'It's Jamie's birthday on Wednesday. We're taking him and some friends to Laserquest and then on to the Pizza Palace . . . '

'Sounds fun . . . ' Felicity turned her head to kiss him. 'We'll have the planning meeting first, then drive into Highcliffe to pick up Jamie — they both stay open late — '

'It's the Easter holidays, and the booking has been made for the afternoon,' he explained, then went on, 'It's just me and Rosa, Felicity. No-one else. Not even Kizzy or William.'

'I see.' The words dripped with ice. 'So your family comes before your future again? Well, you can tell Mitchell

Jarvis you want to cancel the appointment, because I certainly won't.'

'I'm sorry. But maybe Mitchell Jarvis can rearrange for the morning?'

'I doubt it.' She headed towards the door. 'He's booked solid for months. I used all my charms to get Wednesday! Still, I'm sure he'll understand that Rosa must come first.'

'Felicity!' His cry was drowned by the slamming of the bathroom door.

'Oh, why did I have to say that?' Felicity groaned as she turned on the shower. 'You're a jealous, selfish and nasty person, Felicity Phelps!' She glared at herself in the steamy mirror.

Of course Leon had to celebrate Jamie's birthday; of course he and Rosa would be together for it.

'You'll drive him away if you go on like this,' she muttered to herself, stepping into the shower. 'Every time you mention Rosa or the children, it comes out wrong.'

I'm so afraid, she thought. Afraid he'll leave me . . . and there's that other matter we have to talk about . . . Smiling, she lifted her face into the steam.

She showered and dressed quickly, and when she went through she went straight in to his open arms.

'I'm sorry! I do it every time, don't I? You never believe me when I tell you how unsure I am. Please, Leon, don't leave me. I love you so much.'

'I love you, too.' He stroked her hair. Rosa had never needed him this much. Rosa had never needed constant reassurance. In fact, he thought in surprise, Rosa was far, far stronger than Felicity.

'Let's go and eat.' She relaxed in his arms. 'I'll treat you to the best of everything, and you can tell me about Jamie's birthday.'

A Shock For William

The restaurant on the waterfront had only been open a week. Leon looked around him with a professional eye. It wasn't going to offer a threat to the Four Seasons. In fact it wasn't even up to the standard of the Nook. People might come out of curiosity, but they certainly wouldn't make the journey from Highcliffe to Dawley specially. He was pleased. He wanted William to do well with the Nook.

'Any ideas we can pinch?' He grinned at Felicity as she returned from the ladies' room.

'Quite the opposite. Very basic. Our cloakroom facilities at the Four Seasons are going to become legendary!' They laughed together.

'I was thinking.' Felicity paused, her fork poised. 'About Jamie's birthday . . . I know you and Rosa will be giving him a joint present, but I'd like to give him something, too. Do you think he'd object if I did?'

'I'm sure he wouldn't. It's a good idea. It's about time they were all introduced to you anyway. Have you any idea what you'd give him?'

'Well, he's football crazy, isn't he? I thought I might buy him the latest strip of his favourite team. What d'you think?'

'I think he'll love you as much as I do!' Leon laughed, pleased at her insight, and the effort she was prepared to make.

Felicity nodded happily. 'But maybe you should ring Rosa, just to make sure I'm not stepping on any toes?'

'I'll do that.'

She was watching him closely, he noticed, amused. 'What's the matter?'

Laying down her fork, she took a deep breath. This was probably the most important moment of her life.

'I have something to tell you. Leon — I'm pregnant. I'm going to have your baby . . . ' She held her breath, waiting.

'When — when did you know?' Leon was amazed to hear his own voice sound so normal when the world was reeling. The clatter and hum of the restaurant had faded away to the merest whisper.

'This morning . . . ' Felicity gazed at him. 'I rang the doctor from my meeting, but I knew.'

'And — and you don't mind . . . ?' Leon was still stunned.

'Mind? I'm ecstatic!' The joy she felt was impossible to put into words. 'How do you feel? I mean, I won't put any pressure on you. I'm not asking for anything . . . '

'You never have.' Leon sat still, searching the face of this beautiful woman who held his future in her hands. 'But what about your job? I mean, will you want to give it up? Do you want a nanny?'

'No. This baby will give me more than Brennan and Foulkes ever could! I'm not going back after maternity leave. I want to be a mother — a proper mother — to our baby.'

Their baby! The words finally filtered through. His baby — like William and Kizzy and Jamie . . .

How on earth was he going to tell Rosa?

'Leon?' Felicity reached across the table. 'You are pleased, aren't you?'

'Pleased?' He clasped his fingers round hers. 'I'm overjoyed! I'm scared stiff, I'm totally stunned, I don't know what to say — '

'I love you.' The smile shone from her green eyes. 'I love you — and I'm having your baby — and I'm the happiest woman in the world! But you've been through this before . . . '

Leon was whisked back to half-remembered days. The pride and the panic when Rosa had told him they were expecting William — only one year married, and him still a catering student — and living in that pokey flat!

His delight when Kizzy was born — his daughter, his little girl, with her

cute curls and her flashing smile, able
to charm him from the moment he first
saw her.

And Jamie — the one he had
promised would have the best of
everything, because Cookery Nook was
really taking off and they could afford
to live in Honeysuckle House — and
then he'd discovered that although
there was money, there was no time.

And now — this baby, part of him
but not part of Rosa . . . This baby who
would be growing up when he at last
had the time and money and security to
be a proper father.

He hoped his other children would
forgive him.

'Felicity . . . ' Tenderly he reached
across the table and stroked her cheek.
'What will this mean to us?'

'It'll mean that I'll grow delightfully
chubby and be able to leave my natty
little suits firmly in the wardrobe!' She
grinned, holding his hand against her
face and gazing into his eyes. 'It'll mean
moving out of the flat to somewhere

with a garden — trees for a swing, a sandpit, a paddling pool. It'll mean that I'll be behind you one hundred per cent. at the Four Seasons.' She paused. 'Leon, this baby means everything to me . . . '

'And to me,' he said from the heart. 'You — you do want me to be part of this? I mean, you're not intending to be one of those dedicated mothers who don't want Dad around . . . ?'

'Without you, I'm nothing,' she said simply. 'But I won't force you to stay with me. I just want you to.'

'And I will. Always. I'll be the proudest man in the world.' Leon felt in his pocket for his wallet. 'Do you think we could go now? I want to kiss you so very much.'

Laughing, arms linked, they left the restaurant.

It was a mild night, gently warm, with a hint of summer washing in from the sea. Fairy lights twinkled along the promenade, and early holidaymakers were out enjoying the evening.

Solicitously wrapping Felicity's jacket round her shoulders, Leon held her protectively. This feeling of floating delight was a novelty. He had been pleased when Rosa had announced she was expecting the children — but there hadn't been this absolute happiness. Maybe it was because this baby was so much more of a treasure; an unexpected, delightful bonus at a time when he had felt life could hold no more surprises.

'Leon.' She stopped and turned to face him. 'About Rosa . . . '

'You must have read my mind. Telling her won't be easy.'

'You should do it sooner rather than later. It would be terrible if she heard it from somewhere else.'

'I know.' Leon sighed. 'I will tell her — but not until after Jamie's birthday. I can't spoil that for him. I'll tell her after Wednesday — then I'll tell the children.'

'How do you think they'll take it?' She threaded her hand into the crook of his arm and pulled him closer to her.

'I expect William will be philosophical, Kizzy will be disgusted — and Jamie . . . ' He paused. 'I never know how Jamie will react. The other two are grown up and planning their own lives — Jamie's still fragile.'

'It's such a shame that loving always seems to have to hurt someone.'

'That's what Kizzy said,' Leon murmured. 'This — our love — has hurt so many people . . . '

She lifted her face to his and kissed him.

They were still in each other's arms when Lisa and Kizzy emerged from the Golden Garden opposite them. Having made complete fools of themselves on the karaoke, they were giggling and in high spirits.

Lisa saw the couple with their arms around each other leaning against the rails, and grabbed Kizzy's arm. 'Er — while we're still in a silly mood, how about visiting the fairground? I could probably beat you on the Dodgems.'

'I haven't driven a Dodgem car for years! Aren't we too old?'

'Never!' Lisa tugged Kizzy away from the promenade. 'This is the night you banish your doldrums for ever — Andrew Pearson or not!'

'Whatever you say.' Kizzy laughed, bemused at Lisa's haste.

Lisa smiled, thanking her lucky stars that Kizzy had been spared the sight of her dad and Felicity Phelps cuddling like lovelorn teenagers.

* * *

Completely unaware that his daughter had been within yards of them, Leon slowly drew away from Felicity.

'Have you thought of names?'

'Constantly.' She grinned. 'I thought Alex . . . Alexander for a boy, Alexandra for a girl. Alex Phelps has a sort of ring, don't you think?'

'Very nice.' Leon held her close again, not wanting to let her go. 'But Alex Brodie sounds a whole lot better.

243

Because that's what it's going to be, Felicity. Your baby will be called Alex Brodie. Because I want to marry you.'

★ ★ ★

'No, they didn't see us,' Lisa said the next day, as she and William bowled along the motorway. 'They were far too wrapped up in each other! And thank goodness Kizzy didn't have a clue! It cost me a fortune on the fairground but it was worth it. It would have broken her heart.'

'So what did this woman look like? I know Mum's met her, but I've never had the nerve to ask what she's like. Parents! They give you nothing but trouble!'

Lisa looked at him quickly. 'I take it you're none too keen on this little jaunt today?' she asked.

'I'm scared stiff!' he admitted cheerfully. 'Especially after what you've told me about your parents. But if it means any sort of reconciliation . . . '

'That's doubtful.' Lisa shrugged. 'They were so angry about Lewis. Especially because I wouldn't handle things their way. But at least they know I'm coming today, so who knows?'

'And they know about me, do they?'

'Oh, yes. I told them everything. I told them that if they didn't accept you — and Lewis — this was the last time they'd see any of us.'

'And what did they say to that?'

'Nothing.' Lisa lowered her eyes. 'They couldn't. I — er — left the message on the answering machine . . .'

'Oh, great! So we might find the gates barred and bolted?'

'We might. But if we do, it'll be their loss, won't it?'

William laughed, and looked across at her. He loved her very much, this fierce, mysterious girl with her baby and her huge unruly dog.

'Take the next exit.' Lisa looked up at the motorway signs. 'Then take the road to Harbury . . .'

'And is that where your parents live? Harbury itself?'

'Harbury Green, about five miles outside the village. It's very pretty.'

Lisa leaned over into the back seat to tuck Lewis's blanket more firmly round him. When she straightened up, she took a deep breath.

'I know I've always kept my past a closed book, and you've never asked questions, William — and that's one of the reasons I love you. You've always accepted me as I am. When you found out I was homeless and had a baby — not to mention Otis — it didn't seem to make any difference . . .

'I — I won't say anything about Mum and Dad — you'll have to form your own opinion. But Lewis's father — well, I owe you that much.'

'You still don't have to tell me.' He smiled across at her.

'But my parents will assume you know. You deserve better than that.' She turned in her seat and looked at Lewis for a second.

'Lewis's father worked with my parents. He doesn't now, so you don't have to worry about running into him. I don't know where he is now. It doesn't hurt so much now to think about him . . . We were going to be married . . . I trusted Edward. I was so naive!' She spat the word out. 'When I discovered I was pregnant — well . . . '

'He did a runner, did he?' William tried to make his voice impartial. 'Left you to face having Lewis on your own?'

'Exactly.' Her voice was hard.

'And your parents? Didn't they want to kill Edward — or at least make him face up to his responsibilities?'

'No.' Lisa gave a little laugh. 'They didn't want me to keep Lewis, so I left, too.'

'And they never bothered to find out where you were or how you were?'

'Oh, they tried. I made it hard for them, though.' She glanced at him. 'The reason I'm doing this today is because of you. I want them to know that I'm making my own way in life

— with you. I want them to know that whatever happened in my past, you accept it — and that Lewis is a lovely, happy, adorable baby.'

William reached over and squeezed her hand.

They had entered a very pretty, picture-postcard street, with gardens that dawdled down to the soft curve of the road, and crooked cottages that leaned on their neighbours for support.

'Harbury Green.' Lisa swallowed.

'Are you OK?' He squeezed her hand again. 'We can still turn back.'

'No.' Her chin jutted with determination. 'Let's get it over. Turn just here, through the gates . . . '

William looked in surprise at the wrought-iron gates flung wide to herald a curving gravelled drive and a beautiful tangle of willow trees. He drove slowly until he saw a cottage nestled beneath a circle of cherry trees, and brought the car to a halt.

Lisa scrambled to retrieve Lewis from the back seat, while William stretched, his legs cramped after the drive.

The cottage remained silent. There was no mother bustling to the door, no father striding down the path. There was nothing except the expanse of blue sky, the gentle warmth of the sun, and the trilling of birds.

'All right then?' He looked down at Lisa, and smiled at Lewis.

'Fine.' Her smile trembled just a fraction. 'Why did you stop here? Didn't you want them to see the car?'

William looked blank. 'I thought this was your parents' home.'

Lisa laughed. 'No. Mum and Dad are up the drive a bit.'

William pushed the buggy with one hand, the other firmly clasping Lisa's. The gardens were magnificent, sweeping round lakes of grass, dipping away into blue mistiness. His mother would love this place. He saw the house as they rounded the bend. It was huge.

'What does your father do here? Is he the gardener?'

'No. He — er — cooks.'

William laughed in relief. At least they would have some common ground.

'And your mother?'

Lisa's answering giggle was shaky. 'She — er — cooks, too.'

'So that's where you get it from! All those wonderful menu ideas you've introduced at the Nook — are they from your parents?'

'Some of them.' Lisa was bumping Lewis's buggy up the imposing white steps, and as William lifted it towards the huge oak door, while vaguely wondering that they weren't using the kitchen entrance, Lisa tugged the iron bell pull with trembling fingers.

Within seconds the door was opened, and William almost tottered on the top step as he found himself face to face with two very familiar figures.

'William,' Lisa said in a small voice. 'I'd like you to meet my parents.'

'Your parents?' He stared as Lisa's father held out his hand. 'But I — I've seen you both on TV . . . '

Marion Ross, Lisa's mother, reached out her hands to her daughter.

'Oh, Lisa. Can I hold him? Will you let me?' Her eyes shone with tears.

Lisa lifted Lewis out of his nest and put him into his grandmother's arms.

'Lisa!' Donald Ross opened his arms. 'Forgive us, honey? You did such a good job of disappearing. We were so scared for you — '

'I'm all right,' she said, and reached for her father's hand.

'It's all OK now. Isn't it?' Mr Ross said.

'Well, yes.' William grinned. 'She's just told me her parents are cooks. She forgot to mention the prime-time TV shows . . . '

★   ★   ★

'It's so nice to escape from the bedlam at home — I had no idea a few alterations would cause so much disruption.'

251

Rosa and Steven were sitting in the battered armchairs outside his shop. The sun warmed the lane, and the breeze brought the soporific shushing of the sea wafting through the trees. Rosa loved Highcliffe in all seasons, but this had to be her favourite. An ageless time of gentle warmth and sleepy noises — a prelude to the bustle of summer.

Her thoughts drifted to her children.

Jamie, seemingly none the worse for his trip to London, was chattering non-stop about his birthday, delighted with the innovations at Honeysuckle House and apparently now accepting his parents' separation.

She wondered how William and Lisa were faring seeing Lisa's parents.

And Kizzy ... She glanced up towards Steven's flat, where Kizzy was waiting for Andrew.

'Don't worry.' Steven followed her eyes. 'He'll turn up.'

'I know. William said he was as keen to patch things up as Kizzy is. I just hope she doesn't fly off the handle! It was kind of you to offer your flat for the peace negotiations.'

'Neutral ground. Your place is too hectic, and at Andrew's place, his parents would be around. I do remember what it's like to be young.'

'I'm sure you do,' Rosa giggled, 'since you've never really grown up.'

'That's unfair!' Steven's eyes crinkled. 'I'm something of an entrepreneur these days. I've got two businesses.'

'Both of which seem to tick over without too much help from you. The Nook is running as it always did, thanks to William, and this place — ' Rosa looked at the ramshackle shop with its piles of books and ornaments and second-hand furniture. ' — it's about as laid-back as it's possible to get.'

'Just like its owner.' Steven stretched lazily in his chair. 'Don't knock it, Rosa. Who wants to be in the rat-race when you can have a life like this?'

Rosa nodded. Leon and Felicity Phelps could have all the wheeling and dealing if they liked. This slow-paced life was all she had ever wanted.

Even when Honeysuckle House was up and running as a bed and breakfast, she didn't envisage it being anything more than an extension of her family life. It would be perfect. She was a natural homemaker, and she would make her guests as welcome as if they were friends of the family.

Life, at last, was beginning to settle down.

'Hello, Mrs Brodie — Mr Casey.'

'Hi, Andrew.' Rosa squinted up towards the sun. 'Kizzy's upstairs.'

'And she's all right?' Andrew looked as though he hadn't slept for days.

'About as all right as you are.' She smiled kindly at him. 'For goodness' sake get together and sort things out!'

Shooting her a grateful glance, he disappeared into the shop.

'Young love!' Rosa chuckled. 'Who'd want to go through that again?'

'I would.' Steven had pulled his hat down until it rested on his nose and she couldn't see his expression. 'If I was in

254

love with the right person and if she returned the love.'

'You old romantic!' She knew she had to keep this light. She couldn't risk delving too deeply into her own turbulent emotions.

'I've never denied that,' Steven said lazily. 'But love does get easier with age. At least you've made your mistakes, know you won't make the same ones again.' He paused. 'I'd say that middle-aged love had a bit of an edge over young love, all told.'

Rosa said nothing. She had questioned her own feelings over and over again. She still missed Leon, but although she would never have admitted it to anyone else, she could see now how awful their marriage had become.

The hurt was healing, and from that healing a new strength was growing.

'You still miss him?'

'Mind-reader!' she retorted. 'Yes, of course I do, but I don't hate him any more. For the first time in my life, I'm enjoying being me.'

'So are you going to see your solicitor — about a legal separation?'

'No.' She shook her head fiercely. 'Not about separation. Divorce. But I have to tell the children first.'

Steven reached out and covered her hand with his. The gentle pressure of his fingers spoke more eloquently than a thousand words.

Browsers came and went, some buying, some not. People stopped and chatted, commenting on the glorious weather and Honeysuckle House's rejuvenation. No-one seemed to find it the least odd, Rosa thought, that she and Steven should be sitting together. But then, they'd always been friends, and Highcliffe was such a small place — the news of Leon's romance had swept through it like a forest fire.

Rosa watched the smiling, familiar faces as they passed the time of day. They seemed genuinely pleased to see her looking so happy. And that happiness was, she knew, due in no small part to the man sitting beside her.

He stroked her hand, and she turned to him.

'And after the divorce? Do you think Leon will marry Felicity?' Steven watched her eyes. He didn't want to damage this fragile happiness.

Rosa laughed at the idea. 'Can you see Felicity Phelps giving up her Businesswoman of the Year role to become the second Mrs Brodie? No — I don't think marriage is on the cards.'

That the Four Seasons and Felicity Phelps might be the culmination of Leon's impossible dreams didn't even occur to her.

'And what about you?' Steven's voice was low. 'Will you be happy to play the merry divorcée? Or have you been burned too badly to risk another trip into the flames of matrimony?'

'What would you know about matrimony?' Rosa tried to joke. The questions in Steven's eyes were finding an answering echo in her heart, and it was too soon.

'You know why I never married.' Steven's voice continued to soothe her. 'There's only one lady in the world I've ever wanted to be with . . . '

He moved closer to her, his shadow blocking out the sun. 'You smell lovely.' He was so close that she could see his freckles, smudged like gold dust under the weather-beaten skin. 'You smell like new-mown grass, like the warmth of the sun on flowers. Rosa, I love you so much . . . '

She couldn't have resisted his kiss even if she'd wanted to. His lips were gentle on hers, drowsy with love and promise. Rosa returned the kiss in a way she never had with Leon. This was a kiss of burgeoning love and future dreams, a kiss that floated her away on a warm, velvet sea . . .

'Mum!'

Kizzy and Andrew were standing in the shop doorway, gazing at them with a mixture of curiosity and disbelief.

'Oh, Kizzy!' Rosa blushed. 'It's — er — it's not what it seems — '

'I hope it *is* what it seems!' Kizzy laughed. 'Even if you are far too old for this sort of thing! And in public, too!'

Andrew seemed even more embarrassed. Maybe his mother was right about Kizzy's family. Well, it didn't matter a hoot to him.

Steven had watched the censure on Andrew's face and just managed to control his laughter. 'So you consider that romance is the province of the young, and anyone over the age of twenty-five should be retired to carpet slippers and soap operas?'

'Oh, no, of course not . . . '

'Don't tease him, Steven!' Rosa laughed. 'Anyway, do I gather that a truce has been called?'

'Much more than a truce!' Kizzy returned Andrew's embrace. 'The wedding's on again!'

Telling Rosa . . .

'Don't you dare make any comment about the quality of this pizza!' Rosa laughed across the table at Leon.

'I wasn't going to.' He laid down his knife and fork.

'Didn't you like it?' Rosa looked at his hardly-touched plate. 'Or are you still suffering from the after-effects of the Laserquest?'

'I'm not all that hungry, and the laser thing was far more energetic than I'd imagined.' He looked across to the crowded, noisy table beside them. 'But Jamie and his friends loved it — and it hasn't affected their appetites! I must be getting old . . . '

'I can't believe he's fifteen!' Rosa smiled fondly at their son. 'I remember his birth so clearly — far better than the other two.'

'So do I,' Leon said with feeling. 'He

only gave us a moment's notice of his arrival, didn't he? And he's been the same ever since.'

Now, he thought, I'll tell her now, while she's talking about babies, while we're in a public place so that there won't be a scene . . .

'Rosa — '

'It was kind of Felicity to buy him that football strip.' Rosa tore off a chunk of garlic bread. 'None of his friends has got the latest one — it's a definite feather in his cap. I've told him to write and thank her.'

'He could say thank you in person.' There was a lump in his throat. 'It may be a good time for him to meet Felicity. Or would you object?'

'Of course not.' Rosa's laugh sounded brittle. 'After all, she's part of your life now, and the children have accepted that. I just don't want her to come to the house. Not yet. Maybe one day . . .'

'No, of course not. I thought perhaps I could pick Jamie up tomorrow, after my meeting with the architects. Felicity could do him a meal?'

'Ask him. We mustn't make decisions for him. He's got football training tomorrow afternoon — you could collect him from there.'

Leon nodded. 'Look, Rosa. There's something else — '

'Mum! Dad!' Jamie had scrambled from the adjoining table and was beaming at them both. 'This is a wicked birthday! Gary and Robert said they're going to ask their parents to do the same thing, and Simon wishes his parents were like you two. He says his would never let him do anything half so brilliant!' He swallowed his mouthful of pizza and grinned. 'I don't reckon I deserve this — not after . . . well — I just want to say thanks . . . '

'Quite a speech.' Leon smiled across the table as Jamie rejoined his friends. 'And quite an accolade.'

'It's a sad fact, Leon, that if we were still living together, we probably wouldn't be here like this, would we?

You'd be busy at the Nook, and I would have felt unable to cope with it alone. We'd probably have told Jamie he was too old for special birthday parties. We wouldn't have bothered.'

He frowned, recognising the truth of that. He had been guilty for a long time of neglecting his children and taking Rosa for granted.

'Do you know what we are now, Leon?' Rosa sipped her coffee. 'We're friends. We talk to each other about our separate lives, and because of that, we have more time for our children. Weren't you going to tell me something before Jamie made his speech?'

'Was I?' Leon had caught the waiter's eye, and was sorting out the bill. 'I can't remember.'

This wasn't the right time. But when was there going to be a right time? The fragile friendship Rosa had just been talking about would be smashed to smithereens once he'd broken the news to her.

'Dad!' Jamie leaned across their

table. 'Are we going home now?'

'In a moment. Why?'

'I wondered if we could have half an hour at the fairground? Mr and Mrs Beatty gave me some money this morning. 'Mad money', they said. To spend on enjoying myself, because that's what birthdays are for. Please, Dad. Mum?'

They looked at each other and laughed.

' 'Mad money' sounds like pretty poor advice from a bank manager!' Leon grinned. 'All right. You can have an hour from now. We'll pick you up at the entrance dead on ten o'clock, not a minute later!'

Jamie enveloped them both in an uncharacteristic hug, then he'd gone.

Leon pulled on his jacket. 'Well, that gives us another hour together. Shall we find somewhere quieter and have a drink?'

Alarm bells jangled in Rosa's head. He had wanted to tell her something earlier. She had been married to him for too long not to know how his mind worked.

They walked along past the amusement arcade which had led to Jamie's downfall, to the Cat and Fiddle, a quiet, intimate bar.

'What would you like?' Leon found it strange that he had to ask her.

'A tomato juice, please.'

Rosa sat at a corner table, feeling odd. They were like polite strangers instead of a couple who had shared nearly twenty-five years of their lives.

'I couldn't remember if you had Worcester sauce.' Leon put two tomato juices on the table.

'No — this is fine.' Rosa lifted her glass, glad to have something to do with her hands. 'Leon, what's wrong?'

'Have you seen your solicitor yet?'

She met his eyes in a steady gaze. 'I've made an appointment. Leon, I shan't be asking for a legal separation. I shall be divorcing you.'

'Oh.' The word vibrated between them.

'It should only take three months to go through, four at the most.' She swirled the tomato juice round in her glass. 'Four months to end nearly twenty-five years of marriage.'

'As long as it isn't any longer than four months.' He raised his eyes. 'You see, Felicity is expecting my baby in six months' time.'

★   ★   ★

'This makes me feel young again!' Norma Beatty beamed across her crowded garden. 'It reminds me of when the children were courting and brought their friends home.' She grinned at her husband. 'Can you remember that far back?'

'Just about. Some problem up at the house, is there? Is that why they've all descended on us?'

'I'm not sure,' Norma said. 'Rosa's said nothing to me.'

Both William and Kizzy had noticed Rosa's silence when she'd returned from Jamie's birthday party the previous week. But, as Jamie had insisted it had been a totally wicked evening, and Mum and Dad hadn't argued, they put it down to pressure of work at the house.

Kizzy was delighted that she and Andrew had reached a truce when they'd met that hot afternoon at Steven's flat. Her A-levels were now just a stepping stone to her future. She was going to take up her place at the local university, provided she got her grades, and she planned to divide her time at weekends between helping Andrew in the garden centre and waitressing at the B and B.

They'd get married once she'd got her degree, and in the meantime, Andrew and his father would work together and Andrew would live in the chalet. They had beamed delightedly at each other when these decisions had been made, and wondered why on earth they had ever argued.

Life was so good, Kizzy thought

happily, as she flopped down under the apple tree beside the dog and watched William showing Lewis the butterflies on the buddleia. She and Andrew would never, ever make the mistakes her parents had. They would face problems as they arose and tackle them. She couldn't understand why other people found relationships so hard . . .

'I do know Rosa's seen her solicitor,' Norma muttered to her husband. 'I wonder if that's what's bothering her. The finality of it.'

'Could be.' Paul Beatty thanked his lucky stars that his own marriage — and those of his children — had weathered the storms and remained strong.

William dropped down beside Norma. 'It's very kind of you to let us all descend on you like this.'

'Nonsense.' Norma patted his hand. 'Hasn't this been your second home since you were children? Paul and I love having you here. And to see you all so happy! Kizzy and Andrew look like they haven't a care in the world — and your Lisa . . . well, her smile rivals the sunshine.'

'I know. We're lucky. We really want Mum and Dad to come through this OK, so our problems have had to take a bit of a back seat. Still, Kizzy and Andrew have sorted things out now and come to the decision Mum and Dad wanted them to make right at the beginning.'

'Funny how often that happens if people are left to their own devices,' Norma said sagely. 'And they won't regret it, I'm sure. Three years isn't long to wait.'

Three years. William lay back and looked up at the sky. In three years' time, he wasn't sure that he wanted still to be at the Nook, but he would still be cooking. Maybe a restaurant in Cornwall — a fishing village, where they could specialise in seafood dishes. But wherever he was, and whatever he was doing, he knew he would be with Lisa.

'Did Mum tell you Lisa took me to

meet her parents?'

'She mentioned it, but I haven't spoken to her since. Was it successful?'

William laughed. 'You won't believe who they are! Donald and Marion Ross, the TV chefs . . . '

William told Norma and Paul the whole story, pausing only for Norma's little bursts of 'No! Really?' and 'What does she look like in the flesh?'

'So, in the end,' he concluded, 'we parted friends. Lisa's made it clear that we'll be making our own way in life. If they want to see Lewis — whom they cooed over non-stop — she said they're more than welcome, but they can come to us next time. I was so proud of her.'

Norma looked at the pretty, dark-haired girl playing with her baby.

'I'm sure it'll be all right. Imagine, William — you could have extremely famous in-laws!'

'I've thought of that.' He grinned. 'Actually, they were interested in the Nook — and in some of my recipes. They were quite down to earth, really. I

270

liked them in the end.'

'Things seem to be on the up for the Brodie family at the moment. You youngsters seem to have got your futures mapped out. Jamie's settled again — well, as settled as you can be at his age! And your parents . . . '

'Are going their separate ways — which a year ago none of us would have dreamed of. But on the whole . . . yes, I think the worst's behind us.'

'Jamie met Dad's girlfriend last week.' Kizzy joined them.

'And what did he think?'

'Well, he said she's very pretty, and that her flat's like something on the telly! She bought him the perfect birthday present, and it was Dad's idea that he should thank her personally. Mum didn't say much about it — but if she's to be a permanent fixture in Dad's life I suppose we'll have to try to accept her, won't we?'

'Yes, my dear.' Norma stroked her hair. 'And how do you feel about it?'

'Still strange.' Kizzy gave a little

laugh. 'Sometimes I think it would help if I did meet her, because then I might believe it was all real.'

That was probably Rosa's problem, too, Norma thought. Not just the fact that the divorce was gathering momentum, but that the children were beginning to accept Felicity Phelps as a real presence in their father's life.

Poor Rosa. She must give her a ring.

'Is this one more for the party?' Paul looked up, shielding his eyes from the sun, as Otis threw himself into a frenzy of barking and tail-wagging.

'It's Steven!' Norma struggled to her feet. 'Come and make yourself comfortable. I'll fetch another glass.'

'Thanks, Norma. It's kind of you, but I can't stop.'

Otis, annoyed at being ignored, was hurling himself at Steven.

'OK!' He laughed. 'I get the message. You're a beautiful dog! William, have you no control over this animal?'

'None at all!' Lisa pulled Otis away. 'Who's minding your shop?'

'Jamie, and two of his less disreputable friends.' Steven grinned. 'I'm on my way to Honeysuckle House. Rosa told me you were all here, so I wondered if anyone wanted a lift?'

'No, thanks.' Andrew sat beside Kizzy, encircling her with his arms. 'We're going to inflict ourselves on Mr and Mrs Beatty for as long as possible in the hope that they'll ask us to stay for supper.'

'In that case I'll come back and join you. Norma's suppers surpass even the menu at the Nook! See you all soon.'

'I'll walk to the gate with you.' Norma took his arm and, once they were out of earshot, asked, 'What's wrong with Rosa, Steven? She's been so withdrawn. I don't want to interfere, but . . .'

'I know.' He frowned. 'That's why I'm on my way to see her. She phoned me — sounding very odd — and asked if I'd take her into Dawley.'

★ ★ ★

273

'Are you sure about this?' Steven had parked the car at the marina. 'Rosa, won't you tell me what's going on?'

'I can't.' She looked into his eyes for the first time since he had picked her up. 'Until I've done this, I can't tell anyone. Bless you for bringing me here and not bombarding me with questions.'

'Leon isn't here,' Steven pointed out. 'His car isn't here.'

'No. That's why I came this afternoon. I want to see Felicity alone.'

'What good will that do?'

'I promise I'll explain it to you later. Just wait for me. I won't be long.' And kissing his cheek, she slipped from the car.

Steven watched as she walked towards the block of luxury apartments, a small, trim figure in her floating cotton dress, her hair swinging silkily about her shoulders, her head tilted proudly. He loved her with all his heart.

The lift was silent and elegant. Rosa knew Felicity would be at home. She'd phoned Brennan and Foulkes, and that nice little girl on Reception had been so helpful. Miss Phelps was just a bit under the weather and would be working from home for a couple of days . . .

She wiped damp palms on her skirt and pressed the doorbell.

Felicity opened the door, and the smile of welcome froze on her lips.

'I need to talk to you.' Rosa's voice was cold and tight. 'Is it convenient?'

'Well, not really — I mean . . . ' Her green eyes were worried. 'You'd better come in . . . '

Rosa followed her into the flat. It was, as Jamie had said, almost like a stage-set in its pale elegance. For a fleeting moment she simply couldn't visualise Leon living here; Leon, who had a gift for creating muddle wherever he went. How on earth could be live in these opulent, clutterless surroundings? Was this what he wanted? Calm? Peace? A place for everything? And this pale, beautiful woman who seemed to have been crafted to fit exactly with the decor?

With a pang, Rosa noticed his jacket across the back of one of the curved leather chairs. It jarred, somehow. Even Felicity's files and papers, strewn across the table, looked ordered. Leon's jacket was a reality. A sign that people lived here. Lived and laughed — and loved.

'Please sit down.' Felicity indicated the chair with the jacket, but Rosa perched on the sofa. 'I don't know what to say . . .'

'Neither do I. Look, Leon told me . . .'

'I know.' Felicity sighed. 'And I know how you must feel.'

'No, you don't. You haven't got a clue how I feel. How could you?' Rosa found herself reliving that awful moment in the Cat and Fiddle.

She had stared at Leon, then, saying nothing, had pushed her glass away and walked out. Leon had done all the talking after that, but Rosa hadn't heard him. They had walked to the fairground, collected Jamie and his friends, and she still hadn't said anything. There had been nothing *to* say.

Until now.

'I'm divorcing Leon because he wants me to. So don't be concerned. He'll be free to marry you before the baby is born. I just hope you know what you're doing. You'll have two children to look after, you know. Oh, I'm sure you're going to be a very organised mother, but please don't count on Leon. He'll be around for playtimes and bathtimes, maybe occasionally a bedtime story — but the rest of the time you and the baby will be on your own, while he's out chasing dreams . . . '

She swallowed, determined that the tears shouldn't fall in front of this lovely, composed woman who was staring at her with such sympathy.

'There's nothing I can say.' Felicity spoke calmly. 'When we met, you behaved with dignity and I hated myself for loving Leon. Now, I love him even more. I won't pretend that I don't want this baby, because I do. Desperately. I was so jealous of you, because of the children. To the whole world I was cool, calm, competent — everyone thought I had achieved all my goals — but inside, I was shrivelling. I wanted — I wanted to be a mother. A wife and mother.'

'And you will be. You'll probably be perfect — but he won't be the perfect husband and father. Oh!' Rosa stopped, irritated. 'I sound jealous and I'm not! Really I'm not. It's just that I've been through it, Miss Phelps, and I wouldn't want to be in your shoes now.'

'Can't you call me Felicity?'

'No! I'm sorry. It sounds too friendly, being on first-name terms.'

'And we couldn't be friends?'

'Of course not! This is Highcliffe, not Hollywood! I'll never reach the stage of everyone being bosom chums with everyone's past partners.'

To her surprise, Felicity laughed. 'Neither will I. That sounds awful! And for what it's worth, my parents are absolutely horrified. When I told them, they were very angry. It wasn't what they expected.'

'Life isn't what anyone expects, though, is it? And children never conform to their parents' expectations — as you'll find out. The best you can hope for is that they're happy and healthy — and you'll love them, whatever horrors they throw at you.'

Rosa dropped her gaze to the carpet. She didn't want to like Felicity Phelps.

She rose to her feet. 'Thank you for seeing me. When Leon told me, I was stunned, and if I'd said anything at all to him it would have been the wrong thing. I know he loves you, and you obviously love him. I hope that love will mean your baby will grow up secure and happy.' She walked towards the door, and paused. 'I wish your child what I would wish for my own — health and happiness. Goodbye, Miss Phelps.'

The cool aloofness remained all the way down in the lift. The only sound was the drumming in her ears.

Outside, she was almost blinded by the sunlight after the cool shade of the apartment. She could see Steven's car, windows down, music playing, waiting for her. She wanted to run towards it, but Felicity Phelps might be watching. She would retain her dignity.

'OK?' Steven opened the door for her, and she bundled herself into the passenger seat. 'Rosa?'

'Take me home.' She gazed at him as huge, hot tears started to slide down her cheeks. 'Please, just take me home!'

Facing The Family

Rosa sat in the garden nursing a second cup of tea. Honeysuckle House still slept; the builders hadn't yet arrived. She was alone with the freshness of the hour, sun-warmed grass and the salt-tanged breeze. At last she was at peace.

She had cried yesterday all the way back from Dawley, and fitfully through the evening, while Steven kept her company, talking when she wanted to, listening the rest of the time.

He understood her so well. He didn't ask questions, just watched her with those gentle blue eyes, making her calm, giving her confidence.

'You and Felicity have swapped roles,' he'd said, holding her hand as the purple shadows swamped the garden. 'She's giving up her business-woman status to bring up a family. You've raised yours, and are just setting out on this new venture. It's like a seesaw with Leon as the pivot. You've had your share of the downs, Rosa — it's going to be all ups from now on.'

'I think there will probably still be the odd down, too. But I'm not afraid of them now.' She'd gone into his arms, resting her head against him.

He was a comfortable person, Steven. Unconventional, patient, gentle . . . Rosa lifted her face to the early sun. The sort of man she could love without fear, without pretence.

The phone woke her from her daydreams. The sun was hovering above the top of the house. Lewis's wails and the arrival of the builders' lorries added to the noise.

She ran into the sitting-room and picked up the receiver.

'I hope I didn't wake you.' Steven! 'How are you this morning?'

She smiled into the phone. 'Happy — if that's not too risky. At peace with myself and the world. And you?'

'Delighted, now I've spoken to you.

I thought last night's determination might have melted away.' His voice was teasing.

'No. I feel as though I've been ill for a very long time, as if everything was muddled and confused. But now I feel better.'

'Can Honeysuckle House spare you for an hour to have lunch with me?'

'I think the foreman was Attila the Hun in a previous existence! I just get in his way! Can the shop spare you?'

'Definitely. I've got a band of willing helpers now it's the school holidays.' Steven chuckled. 'Jamie and his friends are using me as a sort of commercial training ground before Leon opens the Four Seasons and offers them proper employment.

'I'll pick you up at twelve, shall I? We could drive out to the Globe.'

'Lovely. Steven, thank you — for everything.'

His voice was so tender. 'It's been a pleasure and a privilege.'

Smiling, Rosa replaced the receiver.

Was the old saying 'When one door closes another opens' really true? She had meant what she'd said to Felicity Phelps; she definitely didn't want to be in her shoes. Rosa shook her head. Her life had become so different, so quickly — and yet, she felt she had gained something out of it all.

The builders were crashing about, whistling to their radio. Upstairs, Lisa was bathing Lewis and Otis was barking; she could hear Kizzy and Jamie arguing over the ownership of a T-shirt. Honeysuckle House was pulsing with life — and so was she.

The phone rang again.

'Rosa?' Leon's voice was hesitant. 'Are the children there?'

'Very much so. Why?'

'Because I want to see them — to tell them. Unless you have.'

'About the baby? No, I haven't. It would be a good idea if you did.'

'Felicity told me what you said. She admires you so much.'

'I don't want her admiration, Leon,

or her friendship. I just wanted her to know I wouldn't make things difficult for you.'

'You've changed.' His voice was full of surprise. 'I thought I knew you, Rosa. I didn't think you'd be like this.'

'Like what? How else can I be? No-one can undo what's happened, and I think we owe it to ourselves to behave like adults — like friends. Don't you? Are you coming over now? If you are, I'll tell Kizzy and Jamie to stay put. William's already at the Nook — it's suppliers' day.'

'Yes, I remember. I'll call into the Nook first.'

'I'll have the kettle on — you'll probably need tea and sympathy.'

★ ★ ★

'He's going to marry her, isn't he?' Kizzy said, eyes blazing. 'Well, I'm not going to be a bridesmaid!'

'Me neither!' Jamie insisted, looking

disgusted as the two women collapsed into giggles. 'Oh, you know what I mean! Anyway, I wish Dad would hurry up. Steven said he'd pay me ten pounds if I unpacked the boxes from the salerooms and washed everything. This is costing me money!'

'You're your father's son, right enough.' Rosa ruffled his hair.

She was delighted that Jamie now called Steven by his first name. Their friendship had gone from strength to strength since that awful time Jamie had run away, blaming Steven for the breakdown of his parents' marriage.

But Rosa was sorry for Leon. If Kizzy and William hated the thought of him remarrying, how were they going to react when told the reason why?

'Here he is!' Kizzy spun round from the window. 'I'll let him in.'

'He's still got a key,' Rosa reminded her gently.

'You're not firm enough.' She grinned at her mother. 'You should have changed the locks!'

'I threatened that once. Luckily, we're behaving in a more civilised way now. Your dad will always be welcome here.'

'Not if he wants me to be a bridesmaid, he won't!' But Kizzy was giggling as she ran into the hall to meet him.

'Are you going to stay?' Leon looked at Rosa.

She looked younger each time he saw her these days. She was still wearing the same clothes, long, floral skirts and cotton tops — she had never been one to fuss about clothes. But her face was serene, her eyes clear, and she was always smiling. It hurt to think he had caused her so much anxiety.

'No,' she said. 'I've got a lunch date. I want to get ready, and I think I'll be better out of the way.' She looked at her husband, and then at Kizzy and Jamie. 'Good luck.'

★ ★ ★

'You're going to marry her, aren't you?' Kizzy said as soon as Rosa had left. 'That's what you want to tell us, isn't it?'

Leon sat on the sofa and dropped his hands between his knees.

He'd spoken to William at the Nook, choosing his words carefully. He'd been almost afraid to look at him in case there was contempt in his eyes.

'Congratulations,' William had said, and when Leon had looked at him, he'd seen genuine pleasure.

'You mean it?'

'Sure. There's no point in being any other way, is there? I hope you'll be happy, Dad. Mum's happy, and I want that for both of you.'

Leon looked up into the faces of his two younger children, perched side by side opposite him, their eyes full of questions. He knew it wouldn't be so easy this time. He took a deep breath.

'You're right. I am going to marry Felicity, as soon as the divorce comes through. And yes, there is a reason for us getting married so quickly.' He glanced at Kizzy. She'd guessed, but not Jamie. 'Felicity and I . . . well, how do you fancy a little brother or sister?'

Kizzy clicked her tongue in disgust, then turned to her brother.

'What he's trying to tell you, cloth-head, is that Felicity is expecting a baby. Our half-brother or sister!'

'What?' Jamie wrinkled his nose. 'You can't! You're too old! And anyway, you've got us. Why do you want another baby?'

'Jamie, please . . . ' Leon reached out to his son, who glared at him. 'Listen, you and William and Kizzy belong to me and Mum. The new baby will belong to Felicity and me. It's all part of life . . . '

'No, it isn't!' Jamie jumped to his feet. 'It's sick! Babies should be for young people like William and Lisa. Everyone will laugh at you — and me. My mates thought it was pretty cool when they saw you'd split up and were still friends — like at my birthday. I'd got used to that. And Felicity was nice to me. She talked to me like I was grown-up. I liked her — but I don't now! I hate both of you!'

He rushed from the room, slamming the door.

'Well done.' Kizzy's eyes were cold. 'You handled that really well.'

'What was I supposed to say?' Leon gazed helplessly at his daughter. 'He had to know. Shall I go after him?'

Kizzy shook her head. 'No. Leave him. Have you told William?'

Leon nodded.

'And I suppose he thought it was great? William would. Leave him to talk to Jamie, Dad. Whatever you say will only make matters worse.'

'But suppose he takes it into his head to run away again?'

'Highly unlikely.' Kizzy studied the pattern on the carpet. 'Jamie isn't stupid. He's come to terms with the fact that you're no longer his superhero. The divorce was inevitable, but the

baby . . . ' She paused. 'That's different.'

She looked at her father's troubled
eyes, and relented.

'Oh, Dad, he'll come round. He'll
probably forgive you as soon as you
start advertising for staff at the Four
Seasons. He's dying to work there.'

'Ouch!' Leon gave a wan smile. 'I
don't envy Andrew being your husband
with remarks like that flying about. But
what about you, Kizz? Are you angry
with me?'

'Not angry.' Kizzy twisted a curl
round her finger, the way she always
had. 'Shocked, I suppose. I feel a bit
like Jamie. I mean — you're nearly fifty!
And you're my dad . . . It just doesn't
seem right.'

'Are you pleased for me?'

'Pleased?' Kizzy's eyebrows rose. 'Of
course I'm not pleased. I think you're
mad! But it's your life — yours and
Felicity's. If you want to breed a new
generation of Brodies, then no-one can
stop you, but really, Dad, don't expect

the old Brodies to be delighted.'

Kizzy walked to the window and stared out across the sweep of the gardens. Her life had just settled down — and now there was this!

'Kizzy.' Her father placed his hands on her shoulders. 'Please don't fall out with me about this. I want you to meet Felicity. Your mother has, you know. She's talked to her about the baby. If she can do it, surely you can?'

'You expect too much!' Kizzy flared. 'Jamie's right, Dad. People will snigger and point their fingers. This is a small place! Oh, I know it'll all die down and be accepted in time, but you won't get away with it that easily, and I don't think you deserve to.'

'Nor do I.' Leon drew her towards him. 'But I do love Felicity, Kizz, and I still love your mother — and you. Love isn't diminished by being shared.'

She gave a snort of laughter and Leon saw genuine merriment in her eyes.

'Now you sound like an ageing hippie! Spare me the Sixties philosophy, Dad! And yes, I will meet her — but in my own time.'

Sighing with relief, he pulled his daughter's head to his shoulder and stroked her hair. He hadn't lost his eldest children over this — and he still hoped he wouldn't lose Jamie.

★ ★ ★

Noticing Leon's car in the drive, Steven drove past Honeysuckle House and parked his car in the road and sat for a moment.

Rosa hadn't phoned to say the lunch date was off, so Leon must have arrived unexpectedly. He hoped there wasn't going to be trouble over Rosa's visit to Felicity's flat.

He walked up the drive, skirting the builders' vehicles and the two skips overflowing with debris. The front door was wide open, and Otis basked in the sunshine on the top step.

'Where are they all, eh, boy?' Steven fondled Otis's floppy ears, then rang the doorbell.

Jamie jumped down the last three stairs into the hall. 'Oh, good. Are you going back to the shop?' he asked.

'I wasn't.' Steven looked at this boy he'd become so close to. 'But I can. Do you want a lift?'

'Please.' Jamie scuffed at the tiled floor with his trainers. 'I would have been down sooner but Dad turned up . . .'

Steven nodded, but said nothing. Jamie had been crying, but he certainly wouldn't thank him for noticing it.

'Well, I've sorted the boxes out for you — there's a full afternoon's work there, and if you finish I'll make it fifteen pounds each.'

'Wow! Thanks!' Delight spread across Jamie's white face.

'It's not a bribe.' Steven laughed. 'It'll be darned hard work, even with all of you helping. I really need all that stuff ready to put out tomorrow — this good weather has brought the tourists out, and they're buying everything they can lay their hands on!'

'Don't know why people buy junk.' Jamie grinned at him. 'But I'm glad they do.'

'So am I! Now, are Mum and Dad talking, or is she ready?'

'Dad's talking to Kizzy in the sitting-room.' Jamie's expression was shuttered again. 'Mum said she was ready, but she probably isn't.'

'Well, run and tell her I'm taking you back to the shop — that'll give her time to finish her titivating.'

'Right.' His smile had returned.

The second time Steven parked the car outside the house, Rosa was waiting by the gate. Leon's car was still in the drive.

'You look wonderful.' He opened the door for her. 'It's just as well that isn't a dark dress — the cats have been sleeping in here all morning.'

'I wouldn't mind a few cat hairs.' Rosa relaxed in her seat, allowing the warmth to surround her. 'I'm not Felicity Phelps.'

Steven laughed. 'Put your claws away, Mrs Brodie, and tell me what's the matter with Jamie. I dropped him off at the shop. He was quite chatty, but there was something bothering him.'

'Leon told him about the baby, and I gather he took it badly . . . '

'Of course he did!' Steven steered the car off the main road and on to one of the twisty single track lanes that led away from Highcliffe. 'He's fifteen, for heaven's sake! Poor old Jamie — his world has been rocking a bit lately, hasn't it?'

'So has mine.' Rosa turned her head to look at him.

Smiling, he reached down and lifted her hand, holding it beneath his own on the steering-wheel.

The Globe nestled in the middle of dense woodland, miles off the beaten track. It was set in a mossy clearing and surrounded by gorse and bracken and tall, fronding ferns. It had never been one of Leon's haunts, being far too quiet, although Rosa had always longed to go.

'This is wonderful.' She scrambled from the car, feeling the turf spring beneath her feet. 'You can't hear anything! Just bees and birdsong! This is paradise.'

'I can't believe you've never been here.' Steven caught hold of her hand as they walked towards the low, thatched pub.

'It's never been on Leon's visiting list.' She shrugged. 'No doubt it's been on yours, though.'

'And what's that supposed to mean?' he asked with mock severity.

Rosa slid into one of the wooden benches against the Globe's white-washed walls.

'It means that as you've wined and dined every eligible lady in this county — and all the counties adjoining it — for as long as I can remember, this must have been on your circuit.'

'You do me an injustice.' He sat

down opposite her, leaning across the wooden table. 'When I discovered this place I knew it was special, and I knew that when I found a very special lady, I would bring her here. Sadly, I found my very special lady years ago — and I wasn't able to bring her here until now, was I?'

The silence lengthened. The sun was warm. The air filled with a golden dreamy somnolence. Rosa reached across the table and entwined her fingers with his. His hands were slender and tanned, the hairs bleached white by the sun, a dusting of freckles across the knuckles.

Gently, he stroked her fingers, then caught her other hand and pulled her towards him across the table.

'Rosa Brodie, I love you.'

He kissed her and she could smell the warm, clean scent of him, the perfume of sun on his skin. Then she was only aware of the warmth of his lips on hers and the sweet singing in her ears.

She kissed him back, not wanting to ever let him go; not wanting to relinquish this moment of pleasure, of heady discovery. She loved him . . .

Ages later, or perhaps minutes, they parted and gazed wordlessly at each other. She had never said the words he wanted to hear, but he knew now. One day she would tell him, but now there was no need.

He stroked her hair, tucking a silky strand behind her ear.

'For the umpteenth time I'll say this — Leon is a fool.'

Rosa shook her head. 'No. This feeling that we have — this closeness — could never have happened with Leon and me. Oh, we loved each other, but never like this. Maybe this is what he's found with Felicity. I hope so.'

'You're a remarkable woman.' Steven smiled. 'And I still think he's a fool. Would you like a drink now?'

'Please.' She dropped her gaze shyly. It still seemed strange; this deep and powerful emotion was so new. 'And if it doesn't sound too unromantic, could I have something to eat, please? I missed breakfast.'

'That's right,' Steven grumbled, sliding out from behind the bench. 'Bring me back to reality with a thump! I thought love was supposed to suppress the appetite?'

'It can't be love, then, can it?' Rosa teased him. 'Because I'm starving!'

They ate outside in the drowsy sunlight, sharing a huge ploughman's lunch, feeding the birds that hopped hopefully round their feet. They drank glasses of fruit juice, decorated with crushed ice and sprigs of mint.

They smiled at other couples who joined them in their paradise, but mostly they smiled at each other. The rest of the world and its problems were a million miles away.

'I suppose,' Steven said eventually, 'that we'll have to return to normality soon?'

'Sadly, yes.' Rosa shook the crumbs from her lap to a gaggle of excited sparrows. 'But this will be one of my special memories. Something to be dusted off and brought out to warm bleaker days.'

Steven touched her cheek briefly, before ducking under the Globe's low-beamed doorway to settle the bill. If he had his way, he thought, this would be the first of many visits here. And Rosa would have no more bleak days in her life, if he had the power to prevent it.

He waited for his change, leaning against the bar, and looked out to where Rosa sat in the sunlight. Her dress billowed around her, her hair gleamed, her eyes shone with an inner happiness that had been missing for so long.

He looked at her with love and pride, his feelings painful in their intensity.

'Rosa Brodie, I adore you,' he muttered. 'I'll love you for the rest of my life.'

As they drove off, he reached across to touch her arm. 'Back home, or can I tempt you to a cup of tea at the shop first?'

'Temptation wins hands down.' Rosa laughed. 'I don't want to burst the bubble just yet.'

Again, the warm afternoon had brought the visitors out in force, and the white shingle lane in front of the shop was busy. Jamie, Simon and Gary were happily wrapping things in sheets of distinctive blue-and-gold paper when Rosa and Steven eventually managed to force their way in.

'We've sold tons!' Jamie's eyes were bright with enthusiasm. 'We've even sold some of that new stuff — you know, the stuff I had to unpack and wash.'

'But I hadn't even priced it!' Steven laughed.

'No . . . well, I think I've got the hang of it. I guessed none of it could be really valuable, otherwise you wouldn't have let us loose on it, so I just sold it for whatever I thought. I started at a really high price and then let them sort of bargain it downwards. Sometimes they gave me more than I was going to charge.'

'Brilliant!' Steven held out his hand. 'Shake. Forget about working for your dad or playing football for England. Come and be my partner!'

Jamie grinned hugely as he and Steven shook hands, then he dived outside to chat to a middle-aged couple who were admiring teapots.

Steven opened the till and whistled. 'Your son is a genius, Rosa. I'd just left the float in here — now look!'

The till was respectably full of notes and coins.

'It's worth a king's ransom to see his face.' She squeezed Steven's arm. 'Look at him. He's enjoying himself, and it shows.'

'Like you?'

'Like me,' she agreed. 'We Brodies are very transparent in our emotions, and you seem to fetch out the best in us. Now, I'll go and put the kettle on and find your biggest teapot.'

'Rosa?'

'Yes?' She paused on the stairs leading to the flat and looked over her shoulder.

'Thanks for making today so special.'

'You did that.' Her eyes were steady, on a level with his. 'You always make things special. Steven, I . . . '

He waited, holding her eyes, holding his breath.

'I can't . . . I can't say it. Not yet.'

'Your voice doesn't have to. Your eyes just have,' he said huskily, and she leaned down and kissed him.

'When I'm free, I'll tell you everything. Until then, where do you keep the tea-bags?'

Steven slid his arm round her waist. 'I'd better come and show you. Things never have the same home two days running up here.'

* * *

They had tea and biscuits in the armchairs outside the shop. Jamie and his friends, watchful for potential customers, squatted beside them.

'I don't care about the stupid baby.' Jamie looked up at Rosa. 'I really don't. Do you?'

'Don't be rude about the baby, Jamie. It'll be your half-brother or sister — you'll probably become very good friends.'

'No!' He shook his head vehemently. 'Never!'

'But you like Lewis, don't you?' Steven leaned towards them, balancing his mug of tea on the arm of the chair. 'You're always playing with him and you don't mind being seen pushing his buggy.'

'No, s'pose not.' Jamie considered this. 'If it's a boy I could teach him to play football, couldn't I? After all, Dad's much too old.'

Rosa and Steven exchanged wry smiles.

'And think of it another way,' Steven persevered. 'For the first time you'll be somebody's big brother.'

'Oh yeah! William and Kizzy have always bossed me around — now it'll be my turn!'

'Well, maybe not bossing around so much,' Steven put in quickly. 'More guiding and teaching and explaining.'

'Same thing,' Jamie answered cheerfully.

Rosa smiled at Steven. He had defused this tricky situation in a way she never could have. He really was a pretty remarkable man.

New Beginnings

The sun streamed into the kitchen, shone across the new work surface and glinted on the huge, multi-purpose cooker nestling in the alcove. Rosa looked at it all with satisfaction.

High summer. Honeysuckle House had been offering B and B for three months. Ten full English breakfasts had been served to visitors that morning, and appreciatively demolished. Ten happy holidaymakers had departed to enjoy Highcliffe's beach, or travel into Dawley, each of them full of praise.

Rosa folded the last dishcloth over the radiator and sighed contentedly.

She had been fully booked all summer, and still was until late September. William and Steven were delighted, too, since she tended to suggest to her guests that they should have their evening meal at Cookery Nook.

Life, Rosa thought, was at last on an even keel. William and Lisa were working in the Nook in harmony; Kizzy's exam results were better than any of them had dreamed, assuring her of her university place; and Jamie was spending his school holidays becoming a retailer at Steven's shop.

Rosa leaned on the warm window-sill and stared out across the garden with the ribbon-glint of the sea behind it. It was a perfect morning for Leon and Felicity's wedding.

'Put the kettle on!' Norma Beatty's cry from the back door made her jump. 'I picked up some doughnuts from Parry's on my way. I thought we could indulge ourselves.'

Rosa smiled at her friend. She knew why Norma was here so early.

'That's a great idea.' She filled the kettle. 'I've just finished in the dining-room, and the bedrooms can wait a bit.'

'Isn't it Kizzy's day for the bedrooms?' Norma Beatty unpacked the squishy doughnuts on to a plate.

'Well, yes, but she isn't here today.'

'She's going, then?'

'They're all going. It was the right thing to do. Jamie went at the last minute, under protest, but I think that had more to do with the fact that he had to wear smart trousers and a tie!'

She made the coffee, and Norma followed her into the garden. They sat on the bench looking out to sea.

'If you want me to go, please say so. I shan't take offence. I just thought you shouldn't be alone this morning.'

Rosa reached for her hand. 'No, I'm really pleased to see you.' She looked up at the cloudless sky. 'I feel a bit detached. I mean, I know the wedding's at mid-day. I know that in a short time Felicity and Leon will have the baby. I know all that — and yet it doesn't seem to matter. Does that sound awful?'

'It sounds very normal. And anyway — ' Norma bit into her doughnut

' — so many things have changed, and so quickly, you've probably got used to shocks.'

'I don't think I'll ever get used to them!' Rosa was thinking back. 'If I'd known at Christmas what this year was going to bring . . . '

'But it's just as well we don't, isn't it?' Norma tightened her grip on her friend's hand. 'Life is all the better for springing a few surprises.'

'I think I've had enough of those. I just want life to be boring and uneventful. Please!'

'You've got no chance of that!' Norma grinned. 'Not with your lot!'

They sat in friendly silence for a while. Rosa couldn't help wondering what Felicity would be wearing. Leon would be in his navy suit — the one he'd bought in January to go to the first business meeting at Brennan and Foulkes, when he'd met Felicity . . . There was a sudden lump in her throat.

Thoughts of her own wedding were

310

vibrantly clear. Her joy at marrying Leon, so devil-may-care, so funny, so heartbreakingly handsome — and the sadness that her parents weren't alive to witness her happiness.

The kindness of Leon's elderly parents, and their pride that their catering-student son should have married Rosa.

'A very pretty name for a very pretty girl,' Leon's dad had always said.

Rosa's eyes prickled with tears. At least the older Brodies had seen William born. Kizzy and Jamie had never known their grandparents.

And her dress! It had been the absolute height of fashion for the Seventies. It was packed away now in tissue paper in the loft, never to be seen again — unless Kizzy expressed a wish to wear it.

She swallowed the lump in her throat again, and wiped her eyes with the back of her hand. Wordlessly, Norma handed her a hankie.

Leon had been in the house last

night. William and Lisa, with Kizzy and Andrew, had gone out to have a drink with him. Rosa had refused. It really hadn't seemed right.

And then, when they'd all come back, and she was alone in the dining-room laying up for the next day's breakfasts, he'd come to see her.

'I just wanted to say thank you.'

'What for?' She'd concentrated on folding napkins. 'I didn't buy you a wedding present.'

'Don't try to joke about it, Rosa. I want to thank you for making this so easy for me — for us. You've not once said anything, or made a fuss. You've been the same as you always are — loyal and fair.'

She had looked at him, and his eyes had been filled with tears.

'You'd better go before we both start crying,' she'd said shakily. 'I hope everything goes well tomorrow, and that your trip to Paris is lovely. I hope you'll both be happy and that Alex, when he or she arrives, is as beautiful and talented and healthy as the other Brodie brood.'

'I'll come and see you when we get back.' Leon had stood uncertainly, his hands on the back of the carver chair; the chair that had always been his.

'Yes, all right.'

'And on the opening night of the Four Seasons you'll all come and have the best table?'

'We'll see. I'm sure the kids would love it.'

'Well, I'll go then.' He had looked at her for what seemed a long, long time. 'Goodbye, Rosa.'

And he'd gone, quickly, not looking back.

All this and more was tumbling through Rosa's brain as she sat beside Norma. The shrill of the phone brought her back to the present with a jolt.

'Probably more people wanting bed and breakfast.' Norma grinned at her. 'Paul says this place is a little

313

goldmine. He thinks you should open a chain and sell shares!'

'No fear!' Rosa retorted as she hurried across the lawn. 'This suits me just fine.'

It was cool in the sitting-room as she lifted the receiver.

'Are you all right?' Steven's voice was concerned. 'Keeping busy?'

'Actually I'm lazing in the garden eating doughnuts with Norma! I've done precisely what I promised you I wouldn't — thought of nothing else but weddings all morning. But I'm fine, really. And what about you? Are you going to be able to get away in time to be best man?'

'I'm just leaving. Jamie's pals are holding the fort. Rosa — are you sure you don't mind?'

'Steven Casey! For the thousandth time, you're Leon's best friend.'

'I'd rather be with you, and I'll leave as soon as I can and come over.'

'I know. And, Steven — thanks for ringing.'

'You know why I did, don't you?'

'Yes. Yes, I do. I'll see you this evening.'

When Norma looked up to watch Rosa cross the lawn, she was delighted to see that this time she was smiling.

★   ★   ★

'She looked ever so fat!' Jamie ripped off his tie and threw himself down on the lawn. 'Quite pretty, though. She had this purple dress.'

'Lavender,' Lisa explained, lifting Lewis high above her head. 'Probably cost a fortune. Actually, she looked nice. Do you mind me saying that?'

'Of course I don't.' Sunning herself in the golden warmth of the afternoon, Rosa's doubts and sadness had melted away. 'And it all went without a hitch?'

'Dad messed up his lines.' William smiled. 'I could see him shaking.'

'He did that when we got married, too! He couldn't get his tongue around

Rosa Mary — it came out in a rush as Rosemary.'

'Her second name is Grizzle!' Jamie scoffed. 'Felicity Grizzle Phelps!'

'Giselle.' Lisa was laughing, and Rosa joined in. 'And I suppose it's Brodie now — like you.'

'Like me. And perhaps like you one day?' Rosa said.

'Perhaps. Did William tell you we're going to have a few days with my parents next month?'

'He did. Does this mean that oil has been permanently poured on troubled waters?'

'That's what we're hoping.' William took Lewis from Lisa, and tickled him until he gurgled helplessly. 'We're not sure if it's tactful to mention this today but . . . '

'Go on.' Rosa smiled at them. 'Otherwise I'll die from the suspense!'

'We're going to get engaged on Lewis's first birthday. With a small party here, if that's all right.'

'It's wonderful!' Rosa hugged her

son, and then Lisa, who had so quickly become like a daughter. 'Congratulations! Just what the place needs! It's always been a family home, even though the family is a bit extended these days. And you're going to tell your parents next month?'

Lisa nodded. 'We'd like to invite them to the party, if that's OK?'

'Of course! It'll be lovely.' Rosa grinned at the thought of entertaining Donald and Marion Ross. A year ago she wouldn't have had the confidence to cook for two top chefs, but now she felt she could tackle anything.

'What about Dad — and Felicity?' William scuffed at the baked grass.

Rosa took a deep breath. 'Yes, Dad and Felicity and the baby by then. You must invite them, William. He's your father. It — it'll be fine.'

She walked up the garden towards the house and Kizzy.

'Where's Andrew?' Rosa flopped into the vacant chair beside her.

'Getting me something cool to drink.'

She lifted her curls away from the back of her neck. 'I wish I could get out of this dress, but Dad's asked us to go back to the evening reception.' She reached across and took her mother's hand. 'I wanted to ask if you'd mind.'

'Goodness, all you children are suddenly very solicitous!' She squeezed Kizzy's hand. 'Of course I don't mind. I hope you're all going?'

Kizzy nodded. 'Yes, we are.'

'Did it seem funny — watching him get married to someone else?'

'Weird!' Kizzy grinned. 'Nothing prepared me for the way I felt. I cried.'

'People do at weddings.'

'No, I cried for the past — for all the things that used to be. You know. I'd always hoped . . . '

'I know.' Rosa stroked Kizzy's hair away from her face. 'I know you did. But I knew he'd gone for good. I loved him enough to let him go easily. If I'd forced him to stay we'd have both been desperately unhappy.'

'Do you still love him, Mum?'

Rosa sat back in the deck-chair. Her love for Leon Brodie had been stretched treacherously thin over the years; there had been other near breaking-points. They had drifted apart even before Felicity Phelps.

'I love him, yes. Everybody does. But not with the love that you have for Andrew or William has for Lisa. We grew apart, Kizzy. We both began to want different things. What your father did — breaking away — was pretty brave. I admire him, and I love him as a friend, but if I'm honest, I probably haven't been *in* love with him for years.'

'But what about you?' Kizzy's eyes were troubled. 'It's not right to leave you on your own. Not tonight.'

'Kizzy, you're a dear, sweet girl, but I'm not going to drift around pining and wailing. In fact, I've got plans for tonight myself.'

'Oh, good. Are Norma and Paul coming up for the evening?'

'Not Norma and Paul, no. Steven.'

Kizzy met her mother's eyes, and smiled, and Rosa smiled back.

★ ★ ★

Honeysuckle House seemed very quiet. The young Brodies had all gone off, crammed into a taxi, to Dawley. Lewis had been left with the Beattys, and Otis was lolling on the drive.

Rosa walked in the twilight garden, loving the richness of the scents, and the damp warmth of an August evening. The tempestuous times were behind her; there was nothing now to disrupt her serenity.

She was there to watch as Steven walked round the side of the house, casual in well-worn corduroy trousers and a soft cotton shirt.

Rosa laughed. 'You didn't do today's honours dressed like that?'

'No, I was done up like a dog's dinner!' His laughter mingled with hers.

'How did it go? Oh, I know that Felicity wore a purple tent and her

320

second name is Grizzle and Leon fluffed his lines. I mean, really?'

'It went.' Steven reached for her hand. 'I made a very jokey speech at lunch. I even kissed Felicity and told her she looked lovely, which she did. But she didn't look one inch as lovely as you. I missed you like mad, and I blessed your husband — ex-husband — for being too blind to see what he was doing. So, all in all, it was a very successful day. Have you really been as fine as you sounded this morning?'

'Yes.' Rosa nodded. 'There's been a lot of reminiscing, of course, but a lot of looking forward, too. And I know which one I've enjoyed most.'

He lifted her chin with his forefinger, so that she was gazing into his eyes.

'Good. So, have you any plans for what you'd like to do this evening?'

'None. There's a cold chicken pie and some salad in the fridge, and a bottle of wine cooling. We could eat in.'

'We could, or we could do something

else.' He made a theatrical bow. 'Allow me to conduct you on a magical mystery tour!'

★ ★ ★

The sea had never looked so calm. It stretched before them like a skein of grey silk beneath the darkening sky. There was no wind along the cliff tops, and bats swooped and darted in the warm air.

Steven stood with his arm round her shoulders.

'I'm going to show you Highcliffe as it relates to us. Not to you as Leon's wife, or a mother of three, or even a landlady. But to us, Rosa.'

He paused by the wooden bench that looked out across the sea, where the pines whispered and scattered their fragrance.

'We've already been to Honeysuckle House, where I was made to feel part of the family. Where I watched you, over the years, being everything to everyone, and knew what I wanted you to mean to me. It was here, on this bench, that I told you I was going to buy Leon's shares in Cookery Nook.'

They continued along the cliff top, turning off onto the path that ran down towards the village. The shingle scrunched beneath their feet as they paused outside his shop, and he tightened his grip on her hand.

'Here, as you know, is where I made my first unwise declaration. I risked everything that night, but you just had to know.'

'Your timing was rotten,' Rosa said ruefully. 'Telling me you loved me on the day my husband was leaving me!'

'My timing has always been dreadful. I'm a creature of impulse!'

Rosa joined in the game. 'There was something else here, wasn't there?' She stood on tiptoe and pressed her lips fleetingly to his. 'Our first kiss. The most earth-shattering kiss of my life.'

'And mine.' His gaze held hers.

For more than half an hour they

walked round the village, Rosa seeing it all with new eyes, through the times she had shared with Steven. She had never felt so happy, so contented, so secure. Living with Leon had been like living on a knife edge; she had never known which way his wild ideas and dreams were going to go. With Steven it was so different.

They peered into the lighted windows of Cookery Nook, busy with a mix of villagers and her bed and breakfast guests.

'I hope William will stay on,' Steven observed.

'Oh, I think he and Lisa will for a few years. But one day they'll fly away. William is Leon's son. His dreams will take him out of Highcliffe.'

'And you won't object?'

'Absolutely not. All I want for my children is their happiness.'

'And your own happiness?' He took her hand again as they walked on.

'It's only recently that I've realised I was never in control of my own happiness. As long as everyone else was happy, so was I. But not now.' She snuggled closer. 'Now my happiness is here. Always.'

'Good.' He kissed the top of her hair. 'Are you ready for the next stage? Of course, we'll need the car for that.'

They had only driven for a few hundred yards when Rosa turned delightedly in her seat. 'I've just realised where we're going!'

The Globe nestled in its woodland dell, illuminated by tiny white lights suspended in the trees. Rosa stepped from the car and into Steven's arms.

'We had to be here tonight.' he said softly. 'This belongs to us. Not to Mrs Brodie, but to Rosa, the woman I've always loved and always will. The worst is over, Rosa,' he murmured. 'You've lived through it and won. Now there's only the future, our future.'

'Our future . . . ' Rosa repeated. It sounded right.

Inside, the Globe was softly lit, with pink candles guttering inside golden glasses on the tables. She slid into the chair that Steven held out for her.

'You've planned it all perfectly. This was just what I needed tonight. If we'd stayed at the house . . . '

'Leon would have been all around us. But tonight you're both embarking on your new lives. It had to be special. We had to remember the past, enjoy the present, and then look forward.'

She leaned across the table. 'Steven, thank you sounds so inadequate — but that's all I can do. Thank you from the bottom of my heart.

'There's only one other thing to say to you . . . something that I've never said to you before. Steven, I love you.'

'And I love you. Always and for ever . . . '

His lips sought hers, with happiness, tenderness and delight, and when he released her, they gazed at each other, hands still entwined.

'Marry me, Rosa, please?' He lifted her hands to his lips.

'Yes, Steven. Yes.'

We do hope that you have enjoyed reading this large print book.

Did you know that all of our titles are available for purchase?

We publish a wide range of high quality large print books including:
Romances, Mysteries, Classics
General Fiction
Non Fiction and Westerns

Special interest titles available in large print are:
The Little Oxford Dictionary
Music Book, Song Book
Hymn Book, Service Book

Also available from us courtesy of Oxford University Press:
Young Readers' Dictionary
(large print edition)
Young Readers' Thesaurus
(large print edition)

For further information or a free brochure, please contact us at:
Ulverscroft Large Print Books Ltd.,
The Green, Bradgate Road, Anstey,
Leicester, LE7 7FU, England.
Tel: (00 44) **0116 236 4325**
Fax: (00 44) **0116 234 0205**

THREE TALL TAMARISKS

Christine Briscomb

Joanna Baxter flies from Sydney to
run her parents' small farm in the
Adelaide Hills while they recover
from a road accident. But after
crossing swords with Riley Kemp,
life is anything but uneventful.
Gradually she discovers that Riley's
passionate nature and quirky sense
of humour are capturing her emotions, but a magical day spent with
him on the coast comes to an abrupt
end when the elegant Greta inter-
venes. Did Riley love Greta after all?

SUMMER IN HANOVER SQUARE

Charlotte Grey

The impoverished Margaret Lambart is suddenly flung into all the glitter of the Season in Regency London. Suspected by her godmother's nephew, the influential Marquis St. George, of being merely a common adventuress, she has, nevertheless, a brilliant success, and attracts the attentions of the young Duke of Oxford. However, when the Marquis discovers that Margaret is far from wanting a husband he finds he has to revise his estimate of her true worth.

CONFLICT OF HEARTS

Gillian Kaye

Somerset, at the end of World War I: Daniel Holley, unhappily married to an ailing wife and father of four grown-up children, is attracted to beautiful schoolteacher Harriet Bray, but he knows his love is hopeless. Daniel's only daughter, Amy, who dreams of becoming a milliner and is caught up in her love for young bank clerk John Tottle, looks on as the drama of Daniel and Harriet's fate and happiness gradually unfolds.